THE GATES OF EDEN

There's something inside you that doesn't want to run away, that always wants to return, that saves you from yourself, that makes you what you are, and sucks your blood and caresses your skin and thrusts its stinger into the space behind your eyes.

The trees begin to move and march away, forming ranks and shouldering arms, with flowers falling from the sky and rain like tears that vanish into mist. All the whiteness in the world is going away, to leave you beneath the moon, in an infinite sea of blackness, burning in a sea of tears.

Then the moon goes out, an eye obscured by the lid of darkness, the lid of the world that seals you in. Forever.

And somehow you're glad that this time it's never going to end. ... .

About the author

Brian Stableford was born in 1948 in Shipley, Yorkshire. He worked until recently as a lecturer in Sociology at the University of Reading, but has now returned to full-time writing. He has written about thirty novels, including the much-acclaimed *Empire of Fear*, and many non-fiction books, including *Scientific Romance in Britain 1890–1950* and *The Third Millennium: A History of the World, 2000–3000 A.D.* (in collaboration with David Langford). His sardonic short stories about the biotechnological revolution are a notable feature of the magazine *Interzone*.

Brian Stableford lives in Reading.

The Gates of Eden

Brian Stableford

NEW ENGLISH LIBRARY
Hodder and Stoughton

For Barry Bayley

Copyright © 1983 by Brian Stableford

First published in the United States of America in 1983 by Daw Books

First published in Great Britain in 1990 by New English Library Paperbacks

The right of Brian Stableford to be identified as the author of this work has been asserted by him in accordance with the Copyright, Designs and Patents Act 1988.

British Library C.I.P.

Stableford, Brian *1948–*
  The gates of Eden.
  I. Title
  823.914[F]

ISBN 0 450 53203 8

Printed and bound in Great Britain for Hodder and Stoughton Paperbacks, a division of Hodder and Stoughton Ltd., Mill Road, Dunton Green, Sevenoaks, Kent TN13 2YA. (Editorial Office: 47 Bedford Square, London WC1B 3DP) by Cox & Wyman Ltd., Reading, Berks.

As you move along the corridor the hands sprout from the walls, their slow, slimy fingers groping for your arms and your ankles. The cobwebs catch your face, caressing you, and you feel the eyes of the great fat spiders watching you. They don't move, but somehow that's no mercy.

There are ghosts nearby, but you'll never see them. They're inside the walls, where ghosts prefer to live, coexistent with cold stone. That's your destiny: to wait out eternity entombed in solid rock, moving through the barriers that set apart the spaces where the others live.

The others?

You're one of the others right now. An ephemeral creature; a meaningless dream of the nucleic acids, a sport in the grand game of life. Flesh and blood—flesh that is made to feel pain; blood that fills you up so that every least pin prick will burst you and spill you and shrink you and feed the vampire until you shrivel and fade away and run for cover to the bosom of the cold, cold walls.

The vampire is behind you, and you mustn't forget that. He never drinks wine; how beautiful they sound . . . but he's not like that, not really. His eyes aren't rimmed with red lightning; he has no fangs. He's a

5

creature of the shadows, his face is too frightful even to be imagined. You never hear him coming; but you always know you're caught. It's the feeling of suffocation; the deathly, sickly warmth; the moment when no matter how hard you try, you can't move; you try to lift your limbs but the heaviness is in them; and the blood . . . the blood is squeezing inside its sac . . . squeezing until you burst. . . .

Try to scream!

It's a dream!

Things are not what they seem.

(You know it's a dream. You always know . . . but what's the difference if you can't escape? Waking is dreaming too, but you can't wake from being awake, and if you can't wake from being asleep, why, then . . . being asleep is being awake and the dream has you and won't let you go, and you can be caught and squeezed until you pop like a blister and bleed

and bleed

and. . . .)

It's a shame.

But you're to blame.

What's in a name?

Now it's the staircase, that goes on and on and round and round. The stairs are wooden, the wood is warped, in the middle they sag. They're slick (with polish? with grease? with the wax of candles or dead men's flesh?) and they curve, and with every step you take you nearly slip, but you don't have to come down hard and you can almost float if you will it well . . . float and fly, with your arms spreading and one leg out behind you trailing, like a skater on the ice.

But to float is to yield and to yield is to feel the grip of the hands and the heaviness and the cloud of suffocation flowing up from the depths. The staircase grows steeper and the walls draw in, and you know that when you reach the top of the tower there'll be no place to go, and the night sky won't help you because the stars are so cold and so damnably far away.

The insects that fly by night are as bad as the spiders and the bats which land on your face and suffocate you with their fur while they suck your blood and give you hydrophobia which Pasteur's treatment doesn't cure because there was no double blind . . . but the staircase just goes on and on and on and there's no way out.

No way at all.

There isn't time.

Your number's prime.

Regret your crime.

You hear him coming now, like the id behind the brazen door, the noise like air caught deep in your throat, rasping and groaning, and you know there's no escape.

Even here! You howl (silently) as if it were a surprise, though you always knew, or should have known. . . .

Escape in space

won't win the race

you have to face

it.

You reach out your arms and you try to fly, throwing your head back as if to seek the sun, longing to soar, but all that happens is that waiting hands grip yours, and squeeze until the bones crack, and your shoes sink into the soft wood, which sucks them in, and your feet too, so you're pulled out tight like a man on a cross, and the shadows flow around you with their sickly warmth and their loving touch, all ready to laugh.

It's all a dream, you tell yourself, over and over, because you think if you say it often enough you might spring the doors of sleep.

I want to leave!

I need to grieve.

I need you. . . .

But it's hopeless and you know it. The vampire has you now, and he controls it all. You're at his mercy, and he has no mercy. He can chew you up and spit you out, and you're helpless because, in your heart of hearts, you want him to. You're just a bag of blood, and you need to be squeezed.

For a moment, as he flows around you, you're not quite so scared. But then you catch a glimpse of the face that's too frightful to be seen, and the glimpse is enough to let the terror free.

There's no stemming that tide, once it's burst its banks.

You can't scream anymore, because you have nothing left; all you can do is whisper inside yourself.

It's a dream, a dream, a stupid, filthy dream. . . .

And the vampire opens his red-lipped mouth to show you the darkness inside,
> *and he says,*
> *of course it's a dream,*
> *but it's not* your *dream,*
> *it's* MINE

End of Nightmare

So I wake up sweating. I always do. The sheet is sticky with it, and so crumpled and twisted it's almost knotted around my ankles.

I try to smooth it out.

The first feeling is always profound relief. I've awakened. I'm out of it, back in the real world. Nothing in *these* shadows can hurt me.

I switch on the reading light, just to be sure. I check the pale blue walls, the chromatograms, the hand-colored images of Martian landscapes and Cookham on the Thames. Clean and neat. My heart is slowing down; the panic's over.

Or is it?

I try to remember, and then I *know*. It isn't just the

nightmare. A necessary but not sufficient condition. . . .

It's been so long, but I haven't forgotten, and there's no shadow of a doubt. When it's real, it's real. It's not just worry, it's *certainty*.

My hand is starting to shake, and I take a firm grip on myself. I have to take control. I have to take myself firmly in hand. I can get through it—I *know* I can—if I only go carefully and do everything right. No one must know, but no one *has* to know, if only I'm careful.

The last thing I remember is the stupid party. New Year's Eve. Happy Birthday, 2444 . . . you couldn't possibly tell me what happened to the last few hours of 2443?

I thought not.

It wasn't the drink. I only had one glass. I only *remember* one glass . . . but whatever else is wrong with me I've no hangover. Blackouts don't drive me to drink. Whatever Mr. Hyde gets up to, it isn't swilling alcohol or popping pills. Zeno was there . . . hell, *everyone* was there, from Schumann down. It can't have been more than an hour. What can you do in an hour, especially at a party? Even if I did something *really* crazy, who'd care? A party is protective camouflage. You can do anything at a party. Pretty well anything. Big joke, though, if they caught Lee Caretta off guard. Probably go up six points in their estimation . . . and come down seven when I revert to type.

I thought I'd left it behind me on Earth. I really did. Sule is so goddam far away. Fifty-six million kilometers at the closest pass. You'd think you'd be safe sharing an orbit with a dead world, three HSBs and Stepping Stone. You're supposed to leave lunacy under the moon. *Nobody must know!* Can't be sent home now. Not *now*. I got away with it before, I can get away with it now. If in doubt, bluff. I can do it. I *know* I can. What's an hour of your memory, when you're among friends?

I put my head back on the pillow, not really trying to get back to sleep. I couldn't, and anyway, what's so great about sleep? Sleep is where the nightmares are.

What a way to see the new year in!

End of nightmare?

Well, maybe.

And maybe not.

1

I was sitting in front of the TV, flipping the pages of the latest bulletin, when Zeno knocked on the door. He came in without waiting for an invitation.

He looked over my shoulder to see what was on the screen.

"It's a holiday," he said. "You're supposed to be taking a break, no?"

"You have holidays on Calicos?" (It was one of those silly thoughts that just seemed suddenly odd, for no good reason. Somehow, I hadn't thought of alien beings, however nearly human, having holidays.)

"Of course," he replied. "Even *this* holiday—the beginning of the new year."

"But not Christmas?"

"No," he said. "Not Christmas." He would have smiled, I'm sure, if he could. Anatomy, ever the comedian, had made sure that from a human point of view, he always looked doleful. He had a range of expressions, of course, that meant a lot to his own kind, but by our criteria they only varied his mien from slightly doleful all the way to extremely doleful. It was appropriate, in its way. His view of the world was not redolent with what you or I would call *joi de vivre*. He was dark green in color, with diamond-shaped scales distributed in a tough tegument, and a few eccentric

11

cartilaginous extrusions here and there, but apart from that he was ordinary enough.

"It's not work," I assured him. "I'm just catching up on the latest squabbles between Biochemistry and Taxonomy. We're bound to be called upon to referee. Genetics always has to arbitrate, in the long run. Good party last night, wasn't it?"

I had to admire the way I'd slipped it in like that. I had to begin investigations quickly.

"I'm not sure," he replied cautiously. "It's difficult to know where goodness resides, from the human point of view."

Zeno wasn't his "real" name. It was just the name he'd adopted in order to live among humans. He sometimes said that he'd rather have selected the name of a more recent philosopher, but that "Schopenhauer" was too cumbersome and after studying the implications he'd regretfully declined the opportunity of calling himself "Kant."

"I think I may have had too much to drink," I said. "My memories are a little hazy."

That was playing safe. Always construct an alibi.

"That's strange," he said. "I thought that you drank very moderately, and that you retired early to bed."

I frowned. That didn't sound too hopeful. Perhaps, for the period of the lost memory, I wasn't at the party at all. If so, then where the hell was I? And what had I been doing?

"I see Scarlatti thinks he's got a virus hook-up in some of his mice," I said, pointing to the page of the Bulletin that was on the screen. "More power to the paranoids, I suppose."

Zeno accepted the change of subject gracefully. "I don't think the mice are suffering too terribly," he said. "Last time I spoke to Scarlatti they were in the best of health. Nevertheless, it's a serious matter. Cross-systemic infection isn't to be taken lightly, even as a remote possibility. However. . . ."

He cleared his throat politely, and I remembered that he must have come for a purpose. After all, as he said, it was a holiday. He hadn't dropped in to discuss nucleic acid ubiquity or the progress of the induction experiments.

"What's up?" I asked.

"Schumann wants to see you."

"Why couldn't he use the phone?"

"He did. He called me. He wants to see us both."

For a moment, I'd been *very* worried. Now I was just worried. At least, if it was something I'd done, Schumann didn't yet know it was me. I swallowed anxiously. What on Earth could I have done in an hour, late on New Year's Eve, that could have attracted the attention of the director so quickly? But then, we weren't *on* Earth, were we? We were on Sule, where a man who does strange things and fails to remember them the next morning might be a very dangerous man to have around.

"Okay," I said. I switched off the display and stood up. Zeno was taller than me by about a head. Whether he was exceptionally tall by the standards of his own people, or whether the Calicoi are a race of giants, I didn't know. Zeno was the only one I'd ever met—the only one on Sule. There were half a dozen Calicoi in Marsbase, and maybe three times as many on Earth, but his was a unique position. He was the only alien helping us in our studies of alien biology. He was very useful, not just because he was good at his job, but also because he had a whole tradition of scientific inquiry to draw on that was differently directed than our own. Without Zeno as collaborator, I couldn't have been anywhere near as successful as I was. We were a good team.

"What kind of holidays do *you* have, on Calicos?" I asked, as we walked along the corridor toward the administration section.

"Are there different kinds?" he asked. "I suppose

there are, in a way. They become established by tradition—it is far easier to make a holiday than to cancel it. Like yours, our days of rest are the legacy of the past. Some are religious festivals, some commemorate important historical events."

One could never cease to marvel at the parallels that could be drawn between the Calicoi and ourselves. It was easy to think of them as human beings in funny costumes—caricatures of ourselves. Their world, it seemed, had so very much in common with our own that they might have been the creation of some satirist, except that the satire lacked any significance. Biochemical destiny, it seemed, had neither a sense of humor nor a didactic purpose.

It wasn't far to Schumann's office—Admin was right next to Residential, in the other direction from the lab complexes. Organizers don't like to have to walk too far to work. His assistant gestured us through with hardly a glance in our direction, but it seemed that she wasn't really on duty. She'd just been called in for some particular task, and was obviously keen to get away again.

"See," I murmured to Zeno, "we humans long since ceased to take holidays seriously. That's why we're the galaxy's master race. I bet your lot still take Sundays off."

He didn't have time for a reply. We were already in the great man's presence.

Schumann was going bald, and his beard had long since turned white. It was probably the worry that did it. He didn't look as if he desperately wanted to be in his office either.

"Something's come up," he said.

I gritted my teeth, and waited for the bad news.

"A signal from FTL *Earth Spirit* came in forty minutes ago," he went on. "They have clearance from Earth to pick up supplies here. They're requisitioning food, equipment—and you."

I just couldn't take it in. Whatever I'd been ready for, it wasn't news like this.

Zeno must have been taken by surprise, too. At least, he said nothing. We both waited for Schumann to go on.

"If it's any consolation to you," he said, "we'll be sorry to lose you."

"Hang on," I said, finding my voice. "Since when did Sule become a refuelling station for starships? And when did we become available for the draft? I don't really want to be a crewman on the *Earth Spirit* or any other stardiver."

The director shrugged his shoulders. "Sit down," he said. He was never one to dispense with the formalities—he just took a little time to get around to them, on occasion.

We sat down. So did Schumann.

"*Earth Spirit* checked in with Marsbase the moment she came out of hyperspace," he said. "She also got on the priority beam to Earth. Jason Harmall—he's a space agency exec at Marsbase—will be jetting up here to meet her. He's bringing a woman named Angelina Hesse—does that mean anything to you?"

I glanced at Zeno. "She's a biologist," I said. "Physiology—linked to our field. She's very good."

"Apparently," Schumann went on, "she thinks highly of you, too. She named the pair of you as essential personnel. Harmall requested your secondment. A request from Harmall is the closest thing to a royal command I ever face."

The whole thing had been ticking over in my mind for several minutes by now, and it fell into place at last.

"Jesus Christ!" I said. "They've found it! Earth Three!"

"I think," murmured Zeno, "my friend means Calicos Three."

Either way, it stacked up the same. We had twelve

worlds on the books that boasted so-called Earthlike biology, but only two of them were worlds where human beings—or Calicoi—could walk around in comfort. The rest had no life more complicated than protista, and not enough oxygen to allow a man to breathe. For fifty years we'd been looking for the third world. It looked very much as if I'd hit the jackpot by being in exactly the right place at exactly the right time. Politically speaking, Earth Three might belong to Jason Harmall (whoever he might be), but biologically, it was going to be mine. And Zeno's, of course. Not to mention Angelina Hesse. . . . but I was sure there'd be enough to go around.

"I'm not sure that I understand," said Zeno, in the meantime. "Everyone seems to be acting as though there were some urgency about this matter. Wouldn't it be more sensible to have the *Earth Spirit* return to Earth orbit in order to be re-equipped?"

"Earth orbit is a long way away," said Schumann. "Star Station is on the other side of the sun just now. *Earth Spirit* has to get back with the minimum possible delay. You aren't going on any pleasure trip. There's trouble."

"How much?" I said. "And what kind?"

The director shook his head. "No information," he said. "We've just been told what to do. She'll be docking in thirty-six hours. Can you two get your affairs in order by then? Do you have someone who can take over necessary work in progress?"

I shrugged, having virtually lost interest in work in progress. "You must know something," I said.

"Not about the kind of problems they've run into out there," he said. "All I know is that the HSB that the *Earth Spirit* homed in on was lit by another ship—the *Ariadne*."

"I never heard of an FTL ship called the *Ariadne*," I said.

"That," he said, "is the point. The *Ariadne*, so the

reference tapes assure me, left Earth orbit three hundred and fifty years ago. She went the long way around."

I'd already had my fill of surprises. My mind could no longer boggle. "Well, well," I said, as though it was the most natural thing in the world. "So one of the flying freezers finally thawed out. Plan B worked out after all."

"I'm sorry," put in Zeno. "I don't quite understand."

I looked at Schumann, but he just raised his eyebrows and let me tell it.

"It was long before the golden moment when our two species made the marvelous discovery that they were not alone," I said. "When we first realized that hyperspace gave us a gateway to the universe but that we couldn't navigate in it. We lost a number of ships which couldn't find their way home before hoisting HSB-One. That solved half the problem—but the probes we sent out, jumping at random, kept coming out in the middle of nowhere. We realized for the first time how big space is and how little solar systems are. People got depressed about having the means to dodge the problems of relativity without having any obvious way to make it pay off. Without other HSBs to use as targets, hyperspace was just one big sea of nothing. It dawned on people pretty quickly that the only immediately obvious way to establish a hyperspace route to Alpha Centauri—or even to Pluto—was to transport an HSB on an orthodox ship at sub-light speed. It made the business of opening up the universe a pretty slow and painful one, but it was all we had—and all we have.

"Nowadays, of course, we use robot ships, which we dispatch with clinical regularity from Earth orbit, targeting them at all the G-type stars in the neighborhood. In those days, it wasn't so obvious that that was the way to play it. We didn't know then how very few of those stars would have planets with usable habitats—though we might have guessed that the neighborhood wasn't exactly overpopulated by virtue of the fact that no one else had any HSBs already hoisted. The wise guys of the day decided that if hyperspace was a bust as far as quick access to the universe was concerned, they might as well put some eggs in another basket. The flying freezers were ships carrying a crew, mostly in suspended animation, and passengers—mostly conveniently packaged as fertilized eggs ready to be incubated in artificial wombs. The idea was that they were to travel from star to star, planting beacons but not hanging around. Eventually, it was thought, they'd find a new Earth, and could set about the business of colonization right away."

"I don't see how that makes sense," said Zeno.

"It doesn't," said Schumann. "Not now. But it seemed to, then. *Now* we know that there are very, very few habitable worlds; and we also know that anywhere *we* can live is likely to be inhabited already. Neither of those things was obvious in the early days. We had no standards for comparison. There was a popular myth, bred by a couple of hundred years of speculation, that somewhere out in space we might find a paradise planet—green and lovely and hospitable, just waiting for people to move in. In fact, we thought there might be dozens of them. The idea of colonizing twenty or thirty planets *via* hyperspace seemed out of the question. Too difficult to sustain a warp field around anything much bigger than a touring caravan—too many trips to transport the essentials. Now, of course, if we really did find ourselves knocking at the Gates of Eden, we wouldn't care if it took a thousand trips—because we'd know it was once in a dozen lifetimes. They were hoping it would be a regular thing; far easier to do the trick in one fell swoop. The colony ships seemed to make sense."

"It wasn't *just* that," I pointed out. "This was the last part of the twenty-first century. The time of the

Crash. We were making big strides in space, and stumbling over our feet at home. Earth itself was in a bad way. The colony ships made another kind of sense: they were a kind of insurance policy. Seeds . . . in case the parent plant shriveled up and died. Eggs in more than one basket, see?"

"I think so," answered Zeno.

I turned my attention back to Schumann.

"How far did the *Ariadne* get?"

He shook his head. "No details—but the records show that she never planted a beacon. She never passed through a single system. That means she was rerouted from every one she got close enough to survey, probably with minimum slowdown. Taking into account the relativistic effects, I'd say she may have covered a hundred and fifty or a hundred and eighty light-years."

Known space, as we are pleased to call it, is a bumpy spheroid about sixty light-years in radius. Only the G-type stars within it are "known," of course . . . and not all of them. We could have done better, if we'd only worked harder. More ships, more strategy, more sense. A station a hundred and eighty light-years away—even if it were *just* a station, and not a living world at all, would be a very useful stepping stone.

"Toward galactic center?" I asked.

He nodded. After a moment's pause, he said: "That's all there is. I hate to push when you've just had such wonderful news, but you do have things to do here. I asked you once—can you hand over everything that needs to be carried on within the next day and a half?"

"Who to?" I asked, ungrammatically.

"That's your problem," he retorted. That's how you get to be director—you have to know how to delegate. I forgave him for sounding tough. After all, he was stuck on Sule while we were about to set forth on the Great Adventure.

"Come on, friend," I said to Zeno as I stood up, "the cause of civilization needs us. We are the *conquistadores* of the new Earth." I glanced back at Schumann, and said: "They really must think we're good, if they picked us out of all the men available."

"I don't know about that," said the director, smoothing back the few grey hairs he had left. "Maybe they just think you're expendable."

I laughed. I really thought it was a joke!

2

We got back to the lab, and sat down facing one another beside the main bench.

"What we have to do," said Zeno, "is to decide which projects we can simply terminate, and which we should reallocate. It would be easier, of course, if our writing-up were up to date. There are half a dozen things we should have put into the bulletin before now. Anything which has to be taken over by someone else has to be brought up to date, and really needs supplementary annotation."

"Zee," I said, "you have a distorted sense of priorities. Do you really think any of *this* can possibly matter now?"

"Of course it matters," he said.

"It's junk," I told him. "Slime from some ugly ball of rock. It's an aborted life-system. Evolutionary ABC.

Little bags of chemicals. Sure they have nucleic acids swilling around in their microscopic cells. They have their mutations and their viruses and all the other nasty little shocks that flesh is heir to, but it's just marking time. Nobody *cares* about it. If the entire life-system were to be wiped out by a nova, no one would shed a tear. It's a finger-exercise, Zee—it's allowed us to practice for the real thing, to sharpen our techniques and sharpen our wits. But it has nothing to offer—it doesn't even pose a threat to us, even if some of the lousy viruses *have* found a hook to hang themselves on in Scarlatti's lousy mice. Forget it!"

He heard me out, politely, then he picked up the phone. "I'm calling Tom Thorpe," he said. "He can take my stuff on until they replace us. I suppose they *will* replace us?"

I shook my head, but not in answer to his question. I listened while he apologized to Tom for troubling him on a holiday, and asking him politely if he could please spare the time to drop in at the lab. Tom would spare the time, all right. Like everyone else—including me— he was hung up on his work. Single-mindedness was an essential characteristic in those so close to the top of their profession that they could swing an assignment like Sule. It costs a lot to hoist a man out of a gravity well like Earth's and ship him all the way to Mars-orbit; they always make sure they're getting value for money.

Zeno was right, of course, but I still wanted to take time out to think about it all. This was the kind of thing that we all dreamed about . . . except, of course, when we were busy having nightmares.

"Lee," said Zeno softly (my name's Leander—Lee and Zee for the purposes of the double act), "you don't know that they've found a habitable world—or even a world at all. For all you know, the *Ariadne* may have lit the Hyper-Space Beacon just to call for help.

It might be some kind of shipboard problem—nothing to do with a new planet."

"And for that they need a physiologist and two geneticists who specialize in alien life-systems?"

"Who knows?" he said.

"Sure," I said. "The ship's been invaded by froglike monsters—monsters even more froglike than *you*. Or long exposure to cosmic rays has engendered some frightful new life-form in the egg factory which has started to feed on the frozen flesh of the off-duty crewmen. Then again. . . ."

"Then again," conceded Zeno, "they may have found a new world, with a life-system that's a little weird. Something their own biologists can't cope with, because they're three hundred and fifty years behind the times. I concede—Occam's razor cuts your way."

This is how great partnerships work.

Tom Thorpe came into the lab, and eyed us suspiciously. "Hello Zeno," he said. "You too, Lee—where did you disappear to last night?"

That was just about number one on my top ten list of embarrassing questions.

"Oh . . . you know," I said, hoping that he didn't. Thirty-six hours, I'd be away, and it wouldn't matter anymore.

"Sometimes," said Tom, "I get the feeling that you're anti-social. What's up?"

I told him what was up, at great length. Anything to make him forget the small talk. With Tom's help, we began to work out a plan for shifting most of the work we'd been doing into somebody else's area of responsibility. We gave some to Biochemistry, some to Physiology and some (bending the rules a little) to Pathology. It was all a matter of changing definitions. As Zeno had pointed out, though, that still left the spade-work to do. If the point of what we'd been working on wasn't to be lost—whether our lines of work were continuing or not—we had a hell of a lot of writing up to do. I cheated, and got out the dictaphone. Typing was never my strong suit.

In the afternoon, I tried to get clearance to send a telegram to my mother, but the application was over-ruled. They call it "information control" these days, but what they mean is censorship. Space Agency is sensitive about its affairs. They always tell the Soviets, but never the free press. Marsbase is an independent political domain in all but name, and by no means a re-public. Not even the ghost of democracy. There are reasons for that, of course. There always are. I took time out to write her a letter instead. Bits of it would probably be deleted and there would be "unavoidable" delays in transmission, but enough would get through to let her know that I'd been moved, and that she needn't worry if she didn't hear from me in a while. She wouldn't like it—somehow, during the last couple of years, she'd convinced herself that Sule was just around the corner really, and we got to see one an-other's faces on telecast occasionally. She wouldn't feel the same way about a jump through hyperspace, and who could blame her? It wasn't easy for her—my fa-ther was killed when I was three years old, and for fif-teen years I'd been her sole companion, Losing me to space was bad enough. Losing me to hyperspace was the next best thing to receiving news of my death.

I made it a long letter, and promised that every FTL ship that came back from the new beacon would bring a message from me along with it. She'd grown used to my absence by degrees—first there was university, then assignment in America, then Sule. I did wonder, though, as I signed the letter, whether I'd ever make landfall on Earth again, or whether she'd live to see the day if I did. It was an awkward thought, reminding me of a kind of loneliness that I could never quite put be-hind me.

I ate all my meals in my room or in the lab; I couldn't face the common room, even though I knew there'd be something special on the menu. Usually, any change from the customary diet of synthetic pabulum was an opportunity too good to think of missing, but the circumstances were special. I had the Great Adventure lurking a few hours in my future, and I didn't want anyone else inquiring where I'd been during the crucial hour. Someone, I supposed, must know—but I didn't want to meet them any more than I want to meet inquiring minds which might get too curious about my state of mental health.

When I finally went to bed, I had no difficulty in getting to sleep, and if I dreamed the dreams are mercifully beyond the reach of my memory.

3

The next day dragged as the business of tidying up the loose ends of our work grew more and more tedious and the bits we were picking over grew steadily more trivial and more troublesome. When it got to the stage where I was picking petty quarrels with Zeno in order to have some way of venting my frustration, I decided that it was time to pack up and isolate myself.

I set off along one of the spoke-shafts, climbing the stairways to the upper decks until there was only the ladder to go. I was moving toward the hub of the station, and as I went the gravity declined along with the angular velocity. I always liked that feeling of slowly decreasing weight when I was feeling a little uptight. Lessening the burden of your body always seems to be taking a load off your mind.

The transfer from the spinning station to the "stationary" spindle made me feel a little giddy, and I had to pause at the portal to settle down. Because the spindle was a zero-g environment it no longer made sense to think in terms of up and down, but in my private thoughts I always imagined the docking bays to be "downward" and the observation tower to be "upward," on the grounds that a place where you could look at the naked stars just had to be beneath the sky; to contemplate the awful star-strewn infinity you have to think of yourself as looking *up,* if only because *up,* in metaphorical terms, is the right way to Heaven.

The boys in Astronomy were back at work, it being January the second by our Earth-imitation reckoning, and no longer a holiday. They didn't pay any attention to me, though. They didn't use the observation balcony much themselves; star-gazing and astronomy, they assure me, are two *very* different things.

I floated over to the rail, and anchored myself so I could look straight out into Sagittarius, where the center of the galaxy hid behind its curtain of interstellar dust.

The configuration of bright stars that had somehow suggested itself to the ancients as the figure of a centaur archer was lost in a starfoam sea, whose light dazzled the eyes and startled the mind. It was a sight you had to get used to—some people found it too much to bear, and it made them sick. In all probability, half of the station staff had been up here no more than once, and some might serve a five-year stretch without ever once seeing the naked stars. Some claimed that the sight made them feel as if they were in the presence of God; others that it made them feel so tiny that they were haunted by humility. They had to work hard, though, to cultivate feelings as specific and articulate as that. For me, it was a sensation that didn't translate into any kind of awestruck silliness. It was an experience unique in itself, that didn't need to be compared with some kind of imaginary transcendental nonsense.

There was a tiny spider working its way along the rail, plainly unimpressed by the grandeur beyond the wall, for all that it had so many eyes to see it with. It was an Earthly spider, of course. The main work of the station was to do with alien biology, but we didn't let the specimens run around loose. Plague-paranoia forbade such recklessness, except insofar as Zeno was concerned (the Calicoi had long since served out their period of quarantine). Anyhow, only Earth and Calicos had life-systems sufficiently well-developed to have produced organisms as high on the evolutionary scale as spiders. So far.

I blew the spider off its perch, knowing that it would float around, spinning a string of invisible silk until it caught on something solid. It looked as if it had had a lot of practice in dealing with a no-g environment. It might be the hundredth generation to be born here. I wondered what kind of changes might have been made at the biochemical level by natural selection operating in zero g, and wondered briefly whether I ought to start hunting spiders to prepare for a long-term study. Then I remembered that there wasn't time, and made a mental note to put the idea on the dictaphone. Come to think of it, spiders implied flies—some prey species, at least, maybe feeding on bits of human skin and other debris that collected here. Maybe, I thought, there was a full-blown zero-g ecosystem here, waiting to be investigated.

I looked out at the blazing panorama, wondering where the star might be that would be the sun warming Earth Three. It would be a visible star, I presumed, if it was a G-type less than two hundred light-years away, but it would be insignificant within the multitude.

All the stars I could see were within easy reach of Mars-orbit, through hyperspace, but we had managed to find the way to a mere handful of them. The rest beckoned us with light that left them hundreds or thousands of years before, but in hyperspace they were invisible. All leaps in hyperspace, save those to human-built beacons, were leaps in the dark; and darkness, in accordance with the calculus of probability, was where all such leaps came out. Our FTL ships had jumped into the spaces between stars far too remote to be seen from Earth, and had even ventured into the intergalactic gulf beyond our spiral arm, knowing they could get home again by tracking the glimmer of the HSBs in Mars-orbit. But finding other star systems—trying by random leaps to wind up within a few million kilometers of an alien star—was far, far more difficult than trying to locate half a dozen needles in a haystack.

Maybe God, I thought, *is trying to tell us something. Or maybe he just doesn't like to make things too easy.*

Everyone has occasional attacks of philosophy. Even me.

4

The shuttle carrying Jason Harmall and Angelina Hesse from Marsbase docked in the early evening, four hours before the *Earth Spirit* was due. Rumor flew back to us that they were whisked promptly into conference with Schumann, and we waited in the lab for the summons we knew to be due. It wasn't long in coming.

Harmall was a tall man—almost as tall as Zeno—but he was very slim; his fingers were long and delicate, his jaw deep and narrow. His hair was very fair and his eyes were blue. Angelina Hesse, by contrast, was much squarer of frame and countenance, with serious grey-brown eyes and auburn hair. They were both in the late thirties or early forties—which made me, I suppose, the baby of the party. (Zeno, if you translated his age into our years, was pushing fifty.)

The Space Agency man demonstrated a rare capacity for observing the obvious by asking politely how old I was. I explained that I'd accomplished so much by working hard. He went on to make some equally platitudinous (and faintly insulting) observations about Zeno and the uniqueness of *his* position on Sule. I didn't pay them much attention, and was glad when we could get down to business.

Courtesy of Schumann, we had a genuine conference

table; we also had a wall-screen uncovered, which indicated that we had a little picture-show to look forward to. The *Earth Spirit* had obviously been busy transmitting on a tight beam to Marsbase.

"I want you both to understand," said Harmall to Zeno and me, "that this is strictly a job for volunteers. If at any time you want out, simply say so, and you're out. What I'm about to tell you is controlled information, and I'll have to ask you not to repeat any of it for the time being—that's just a formality. What needs to be said now is that the job is dangerous; maybe very dangerous. I have to know whether you're prepared to accept that. Dr. Caretta?"

"I'm in," I said, unhesitatingly. It's easy to be brave when you're talking in abstractions.

He only had to glance at Zeno, who nodded calmly.

"Well then, I'll be brief. Captain D'Orsay, late of the *Ariadne*, is coming in on the *Earth Spirit*, and she can provide full details of the whole story. The *Ariadne* was targeted at a star-cluster a hundred and forty to a hundred and fifty light-years or so toward galactic center. There are something on the order of forty stars in the cluster, over half of them G-type. In getting there she made close enough passage to two other stars to be able to survey them for possible Earthlike planets, but drew a blank.

"*Ariadne*, as you know, is a colony-ship, carrying three crews in suspended animation. Officers were awakened periodically to carry out systems checks and to evaluate incoming information.

"Once into the cluster, she hit an apparent jackpot. The evidence suggests that at least ten of the G-types have planetary systems, and the odds seem good that at least half of those have life-supporting planets. *Ariadne* headed straight for the likeliest prospect, and found *this*."

Schumann dimmed the lights, and Harmall dabbed at a button on the screen with one of his long fingers.

It was a still picture, not a video-tape, but it looked as sharp now as when it was taken

Earth, from space, looks blue with lots of white streaks. The continents never really show up very well, and they always look rather undistinguished—mottled and muddy—by comparison with the smooth, bright ocean. *This* world, by contrast, was mostly green-and-white. The clouds might have been Earthly clouds, white and voluminous. The *other* "Earthlike" worlds don't have clouds like that. They either have a green-house atmosphere that is mottled in shades of grey without a break, or they have hardly anything at all. The surface below the clouds, if it really *was* land, appeared to be highly verdant. If there was water there, it must have been a virtual soup of photosynthetic algae.

Out of the corner of my eye I caught a glimpse of Angelina Hesse. She was watching me. Clearly, she'd already seen the peep-show.

"It's a very similar kind of world to our own," said Harmall. "Apparently, though, it's more stable. Less axial tilt, a trifle smaller, with a shorter day. A single moon, but much smaller than our own—less influential in terms of tides. Little evidence of tectonic activity and no noticeable vulcanism. Not much in the way of mountains; the seas are shallow and there are vast shallow swamps covering fully half the planetary surface. What you or I would call solid ground accounts for only a seventh of the surface, not counting islands in the swamplands, which are legion. No deserts, but there are polar ice-fields which—of course—are hidden here by cloud cover. The name given to it by the duty-crew is Naxos."

"Why?" I inquired.

"Naxos," explained Harmall, "was the island where Ariadne was abandoned by Theseus, and from which she was subsequently rescued by Dionysus, who gave her a place among the stars."

I wasn't altogether convinced of the propriety of that, but it was hardly for me to question it.

"One full crew was revived," the blond man went on. "Captain d'Orsay, following the procedure laid down, floated a technical crew down to the surface. There they established a bubble-dome, following the rules with regard to sterile environments. The dome was completely sealed, with a space between the two membranes of the shell that could be evacuated, with a double airlock and the usual facilities for showering down. No one went outside, of course, without a sterile suit. This ground-crew consisted of twenty people. A reserve of thirty waited aboard ship. Six of the twenty were ecosystemic analysts, but as you can imagine, they'd had no opportunity to develop the experience that is routinely available nowadays. Similarly, their equipment was crude compared to what we can put into the field.

"All the early results implied that the planet was both habitable and safe. The one obvious danger was oxygen intoxication: the partial pressure of oxygen in the atmosphere at ground level is a little higher on Naxos than on Earth. They found no obvious evidence of biological threat. They found that the basis of the life-system was a nucleic acid similar to DNA, and that the supplementary cell biochemistry was a reasonable analogue of our own. They worked, of course, mostly with plant specimens, and they carried out their work with all due precautions—at least, we *suppose* that they did. In view of what happened, there must be some doubt. Perhaps they got careless when nothing showed up to worry them."

He paused, and began to prod the button under the screen again. The green world disappeared, to be replaced by a series of shots taken on the planet's surface. All stills. Long-shots and close-ups, mixed in together. Stands of trees, individual flowering plants, flat expanses of tall grass. Ponds and streams decked out with rafts of vegetation or trailing pennants of weed. Insects ranging from small, rounded bugs to big dragonflies, with chimerical water-beasties thrown in for good measure. A few creatures that wore their skeletons inside instead of out, but none bigger than my hand, mostly soft and moist of skin—nothing that could properly be insulted if you decided to call it a frog.

There were half a dozen points in the sequence where I wanted to call "stop," but I let the chances go. There'd be other times. FTL journeys are notoriously boring—what's there to do in zero-*g* but study hard?

Then the pictures changed to interior shots. The dome and its staff. People at work and people at rest. The lab, where everyone wore plastic bags and polythene festoons made the whole working area into a parody of a membrane-filled cell. Chromatograms by the dozen, plotting out in pastel-colored clouds the chemical make-up of the not-so-very-alien life-system. White mice, unprotected by plastic bags, running free and waiting (though they surely didn't know it!) to give warning of any pathogens by falling ill and maybe dying. Canaries, too, testing the local seeds for digestibility. The mice and the canaries looked suspiciously healthy, bearing in mind the baleful comments Harmall had appended to his last instalment of the Naxos saga.

The show finished without offering the least pictorial evidence of anything going wrong. The lights came on again.

"Well?" I said to the man from the Space Agency.

"They blew it," he said. "They all died. Every last one, within the space of a single night. They never got a chance to find out what it was that hit them. They couldn't provide the shipboard personnel with a single clue. They started dying, and they had no way to fight."

"Cross-systemic infection," I said. "Instant epidemic. That's what you think?"

"I don't know what to think," replied Harmall. "That's up to you, if you want the job."

"Nobody else went down from the ship?"

Harmall shook his head. "By this time, the crew had the HSB in orbit and ready to burn. Captain d'Orsay considered that a state of emergency had arisen. The captains of the other crews were revived, and d'Orsay handed over command to Captain Juhasz. Rather than send a second technical crew to follow the first, he decided to wait for a time for a response to the beacon. He considered—correctly—that three hundred and fifty years of technical progress and expanding knowledge might allow him to call upon greater resources than he already had on the *Ariadne*. All further investigation of the surface was carried out by robot probes—which were not, of course, permitted to return."

"We three, then, are being invited to play detective?" This time the question came from Zeno.

"That's right," said Harmall. "As I've said, there are manifest dangers. On the other hand, you start with one advantage: the bodies are there for examination. An autopsy might reveal the cause of death. Forewarned is forearmed."

"How long will they have been dead by the time we get there?" I wanted to know.

"Nearly two months," he told me.

Obviously, it wasn't going to be a nice job. On the other hand, I was only a humble geneticist. Angelina Hesse was a physiologist. In my book, that made her number-one scalpel-wielder. Zeno and I were the hit men—we had to sort out the cure once the disease was identified.

"Why no pathologist?" I inquired.

"There is one," said Harmall. "He's coming in from a station in the belt."

"A Soviet?"

"That's right. Vesenkov—know him?"

I shook my head. Theoretically, the principle of freedom of information applies to research findings in pure science. For a while, I'd actually bothered to keep up with the bulletins published in English by the Soviets, but I'd eventually realized that they were never going to tell me anything non-trivial that I didn't already know. Whether acknowledged or not, the principle of sovereignty extended to knowledge as well as to territory. We probably had agents who knew everything that appeared in the Soviets' own bulletins, just as they had agents who read ours in the original, but information like that doesn't filter back to the poor sods who do all the work.

"This is a matter for the concern of the entire race," said Harmall smoothly. "We're obliged to permit a Soviet observer to participate in our investigations. We asked them to supply a competent professional, and they of course agreed. He'll be here in two days. The *Earth Spirit* should be just about ready to set out by then, assuming that you can have your equipment stowed quickly enough. You can discuss weight and size restrictions with the quartermaster. Are you still with us?"

I was still with him. It had never crossed my mind to consider the possibility of backing out. Obviously, the *Ariadne*'s team had made a mistake. I thought of myself as the kind of man who never made mistakes. Ergo, I figured, there was nothing to be scared of.

I broached what seemed to me, at the time, to be a much more important question. "On the basis of what you've shown us," I said, "Naxos isn't as . . . well-developed . . . as Earth. In an evolutionary sense, that is. All the vertebrates in those pictures are what we'd call primitive. Amphibious. The implication is that the cleidoic egg hasn't yet appeared, nor internal temperature regulation as in Earthly mammals. I take it from what you said earlier that such a state of affairs wouldn't be too surprising—climatic stability and an abundance of water seem to be the rule there. Am I right?"

"There is no evidence of creatures resembling mammals," he replied. "Our information is very limited, though. We would hesitate to make statements about the whole world on the basis of what was discovered in one locality in a matter of twenty days."

"You have supplementary evidence from the robots."

"Very little," he said.

He was playing coy. It wasn't just scientific caution. For some reason, he didn't *want* to jump to the oh-so-attractive conclusion that Naxos was a virgin world, ready for exploitation if only it could be demonstrated that humans *could* live there. Maybe, I thought, it was an official line, chosen so as to provide an excuse for holding the Soviets back from a more intimate involvement. If Naxos *was* what it seemed, then it surely was a matter to interest the whole human race; but while we could treat it as nothing more than another biological puzzle, with no real practical implications, it would be much easier for Space Agency to keep control.

I didn't bother to follow up the line of thought. It didn't really interest me that much.

"Have we finished for the time being?" asked Schumann.

Harmall signaled that we had, though he looked around once more to see if there was any sign of anyone wanting to back out.

"In that case," said the director, "you'd better take Dr. Hesse to your lab, Lee. No equipment came up from Marsbase, and I doubt if Vesenkov will bring any from the Belt. You'd better start deciding what you need, before the *Earth Spirit*'s quartermaster begins telling you what you can't have."

I was the last to leave the room, and as I looked back at Schumann, he said, "Good luck." I realized then that he had meant the remark about being expendable.

"You don't really think there's something there that we can't handle, do you?" I asked him.

"Why do you think Zeno is included?" he countered. His voice was low. Zeno was out in the corridor, moving away.

"He and I are a good team?" I suggested.

"A bug which knocks out humans just like *that*," he said, snapping his fingers, "might take a little longer to dispose of a Calicoi. Or maybe it will work the other way around. Either way, someone could be on hand to watch it happen, and get the story back. *That*'s how dangerous Harmall thinks it is."

"You worry too much," I told him.

Directors are paid to be cautious to the point of paranoia. *I* preferred to think that Zeno was in for much the same reason that Vesenkov was in—because the Calicoi had every right to take an interest in the *Ariadne*'s discovery.

"Well," he said, "good luck anyway."

"Thanks," I replied. "I'll tell you the whole story, next time I pass this way."

I figured that I was in a position to be generous with my promises.

5

When they told me that the Department had decided to throw a party to bid us farewell, I was not exactly overjoyed. Indeed, I felt a distinct sinking feeling in my stomach. I could hardly refuse, though; it wouldn't have done any good, and it would have offended a lot of people. So close to New Year's Eve, it couldn't actually be said that they needed another excuse to let their hair down, but on the other hand, when you're so many millions of miles from home, who can say that they *didn't* need it?

As always, they took the partition walls down to increase the size of the common room and make room for a dance floor. Out there, the lights were dim and colored, and they had a couple of strobes set up. I decided that I wasn't going near them. It was unlikely that my blackout had been caused by strobes interfering with my alpha rhythms, but I was damn certain that I wasn't going to take the chance. I elected to stay in the brightly lit space behind the bar area, sipping the indigenous brew that the non-pedantic members our fraternity were pleased to call "wine." I tried to look as if I was enjoying myself, just in case anybody cared. If challenged, I reckoned that I could always excuse my unease by explaining how sorry I was to leave good old Sule, which was a home from home to me.

A few people drifted up to me to offer me their good wishes and ask polite but inquisitive questions about where I might be going and why. They weren't upset when I explained why I couldn't answer them.

I was just wondering how long I ought to stick it out before tendering my apologies and pleading lack of sleep, when I was accosted by a woman I didn't know. She was about fifty, with short-cropped grey hair, and looked rather like my mother's older sister.

"Dr. Caretta?" she asked.

"I'm Lee Caretta," I confirmed. There was something about the situation which was vaguely alarming, but I couldn't quite figure out what.

"I'm Catherine d'Orsay," she said.

I nodded vaguely, and it wasn't until a half-frown crossed her face that it sunk in.

"D'Orsay!" I exclaimed. "You're the Captain of the. . . ."

"Not anymore," she said, swiftly and flatly. "I handed over the command."

My mouth was still open and moving, but no sound came out. It was easy to see that she didn't want to pursue the matter. I cast around for some other approach.

"You don't look old enough to be my fourteen times great-grandmother," I observed, wishing after I said it that it didn't seem so snide.

She was up to it, though. "You don't look old enough to be one of the top men in your field," she countered.

"You know how it is," I said, piling gaffe upon gaffe. "These days, if you don't make your mark before you're thirty, you never will."

She let that one die the death it deserved. After a suitable pause, she said, "Do you mind if I talk to you—somewhere where we don't have to compete with the music?"

I put my plastic cup down on a shelf, and wiped my

hand on the back of my trousers because a little of the fluid had somehow spilled on to my fingers.

"Sure," I said. "We can slip into sick bay. It's just down the corridor and it's always quiet when nobody's ill."

There was a half-frown again, as if she didn't think the sick bay was entirely appropriate, but she nodded. As we went out of the door I inclined my head back in the direction of the frenetic festivity.

"Hasn't changed much since your time, I guess?"

"No," she said. "That's the most alarming thing about these last few days. Everything is so tediously familiar."

"Wouldn't have been *too* different if it were seven hundred years ago," I observed. "Except that we wouldn't be on a space station and we'd have funny costumes on. Dancing and drinking are the hardy perennials of human behavior."

"And sex," she added drily.

"Yes," I answered. "That too."

"If I'd stepped out of 1744 into the twenty-first century," she said, "I'd notice plenty of differences. But from the twenty-first to the twenty-fifth. . . . I keep on looking, but I'm damned if I can find them."

I opened the door of the sick bay, and stood aside to let her go through. She looked at the beds draped with plastic curtains, and moved to the main desk. She took the chair from behind it; I borrowed one from beside the nearest bed.

"There are reasons for that," I said, referring to the lack of perceptible changes in the human condition.

"So I've heard," she replied.

"What can I do for you?"

"You can help me out with a few explanations."

I raised my eyebrows, signaling: *Why me?*

"I've already tried Harmall," she said. "I've also talked to your boss, Schumann. I keep getting stalled. The secretive voice of authority."

"What makes you think I'll tell you anything they won't? What makes you think I *can*?"

"I daresay you can't," she said. "And that might be the advantage I need. If you don't know, you have to guess—and guesses aren't secret, are they?"

"For the very good reason that they might not be right."

She shrugged. "Why won't they let me go to Earth?" She fired the question at me like a rifle shot.

"Maybe they need you aboard the *Earth Spirit* on the trip back to your brand new HSB," I suggested. "Harmall did sort of promise us a fuller briefing on the situation as viewed from the *Ariadne*."

"There are plenty of people aboard the *Ariadne* who could brief you on arrival," she said. "You'd want to look over the data yourselves, anyhow. I wasn't planning to go back; I was planning to carry the news all the way home. And I was planning to do my talking to a lot more people—and a lot more important people—than Jason Harmall. As things stand, I don't even know if anyone on Earth even knows that the *Ariadne* reached her target."

"They'll know," I assured her. "They just might not want it to become common knowledge. Information control."

"That," she said, "is what needs explaining. You're telling me that the finding of Naxos isn't going to be publicized—that the whole affair is going to be handled in secret by a select group of politicians and scientists?"

"That's right," I told her. "Does that surprise you?"

"Not really," she answered, with the ghost of a sigh. "But I was rather hoping that I might be surprised, if you see what I mean."

I nodded.

"Tediously familiar," she said. "Every way I turn. There's still a Soviet bloc, I hear, and they're still 'they' while we're 'us.' I really do find that very hard to swal-

low, after all this time. It seems as though the whole
solar system has been in suspended animation, right
along with me."

I found a paper clip, and began studiously unwinding it. Rumor has it that paper clips go all the way
back to the days of the Roman Empire, except that
there wasn't any paper then. Parchment clips, I suppose they'd be. Similar in design, anyhow.

"Not far wrong, I suppose," I told her. "You'd have
set sail on the great starry sea during the early generations of the Crash, I guess. I never was much good at
dates. It wasn't really a crash—more a kind of slow
fizzle. The world failed to end, with either a bang or a
whimper. It just descended into a kind of torpor. A
failure of the agricultural base, spread over six or seven
generations. No one cause—just a gradual unwinding
of the ecosystem's balancing mechanism. A couple of
wars and their aftermath helped, but they weren't crucial. Deforestation, soil exhaustion, pollution—they
were what did it, by degrees. The fossil fuels never ran
out, oddly enough, but getting them out of the ground
. . . that was something else. Mining and industry continued as best they could, but the primary production
system went slowly to hell, and took everything else
along with it. There was a forced rethinking of priorities. The green machine broke down and the only effort that made any sense was trying to get it working
again. They failed. They just had to wait until it re-
paired itself. A lot of people died . . . not all at once,
as if there were a second deluge or a great plague, but
one by one, here and there, a decade or two before
their time. Famine spread, until it wasn't just in Africa
and Southeast Asia anymore, but in everybody's back
yard. Everybody—whether he was a Latin American
peasant or a citizen of New York, had to start thinking
about cultivating his garden—literally.

"There's a kind of irony, I suppose, that everyone
had thought of the ecosystem as something wonderful

and eternal, and of the political system as something transient and arbitrary. You might think that during the century of the greenhouse effect, when the climate temporarily went crazy, the first thing to go would be the governments of the day, their bureaucracies and their ideologies. Not a bit of it—they endured, with astonishing tenacity. There were revolutions, and invasions, and all the usual routine things like that, but at the end of the day the map looked pretty much as it had done at the beginning. Carbon dioxide levels in the atmosphere escalated, and it got hotter for a while, but it was surprisingly short lived—we can say this with equanimity now, I guess, though people down there in those days spent their entire lifetimes being surprised. The ecosystem *did* regenerate, without our doing anything conspicuous to help it except try to stop hurting it. I suppose that on Earth, they're just about back to where they were in the early twenty-first century, which is not bad considering. But we *have* had three hundred and fifty years, or thereabouts, when we had to put the very possibility of progress on the shelf, insofar as it depended on Earthly events. Not much went on in the way of research, practical *or* theoretical, as you'll probably understand. There is a school of thought, mind you, who say that the Crash didn't make much difference anyway—that we were already close to the end of progress, at least in theory, simply because we'd already induced just about all that we *can* induce, given the limits of the human sensorium.

"Having said all that, though, there's one other point that needs to be mentioned, and that is that one tiny segment of the human race has stood rather to one side of all the troubles. Out here in space, things always looked different. Not that the various habitats in space were ever genuinely independent of Earth—but no matter how short the peasants went, the spacemen always got *theirs*. They didn't need so very much, as things turned out, and they could provide a good deal in return—mostly beamed-down power, but even apart from that, the people on Earth were always prepared to give the spacers priority. I think you must know more than I do about the mentality behind that."

"And progress went on the shelf out in space, too?" she queried.

"That depends what kind of progress you mean," I said. "Mostly, I'd say yes. There was nothing like Sule a hundred years ago, or even fifty. A research establishment in space was something really strange even when I was at school. The progress they made out here through those long centuries of hardship was simply physical progress. They built things. They gradually extended the human domain. New stations, new ships. All the time, of course, they never stopped looking for new worlds, but we'd grown just a little cynical about that particular dream in recent years."

She was silent for a few minutes, thinking it over. I let her think. I'd gone on long enough. I was wishing now that I'd brought my drink with me from the party. My throat felt dry.

"So there's still a Soviet bloc," she said. "And there's still a free world."

"It's a little bit more complicated than that," I said. "It always was."

"There's not much real antagonism between them," I said. "For all that they have different laws concerning ownership, and for all that they still attack one another's philosophies in the interests of maintaining their own social solidarity, they get along all right. At least, the Soviets-in-space get along well enough with our-side-in-space. There's another dimension of 'us' and 'them' now. There's *us*—and there's the ones down the bottom of the big well."

"Well?"

"Gravity well. Earth is the big well. Mars is the little one."

"Yes," she said, "of course. And who exactly is it

that is so concerned with maintaining secrecy? Is it us—or is it *us*?"

"I don't know."

"Or care?"

"There's no payoff in caring. I try to live with it. There's a school of thought which holds that post-Crash civilization is wiser than pre-Crash because no one expects things to be perfect. We've all accepted, so it's said, that we live in an imperfect world, and always will. Idealism and hedonism, it's said, have both declined markedly since their heyday."

"You keep saying: 'So it's said.' Don't you believe it?"

"How do I know what it was like in the olden days? You tell me."

"I would," she assured me, "if only I could look long enough to find out."

"You don't really need me to tell you all this," I said. "There are all kinds of history tapes in the datastore. You could get a blow-by-blow account of the whole thing."

"I could," she said. "But tapes don't necessarily select things in accordance with what the inquiring mind wants or needs to know. And tapes don't make guesses."

"Neither do I," I told her.

"Do you trust Jason Harmall?" she fired at me.

"No one's asked me to," I countered.

"*Would* you trust him?"

"I don't trust anyone," I said. "Except my mother. And maybe Zeno. But he looks like a bit of a bastard to me, if that's what you're angling for. Why?"

"Dr. Caretta," she said softly, "I've been on a journey of three hundred and fifty years, across the big desert of empty space. I've aged over ten years, lived in short stretches of ten and fifteen weeks. I did all that because I believed, passionately, in what the *Ariadne* was *for*. I sometimes get the impression that no one

here really cares what the *Ariadne* was for, and that
I'm being prevented from getting through to people
who might. I want the *Ariadne*'s mission to be completed. Jason Harmall isn't going to stop me. I'm looking to you for help . . . you have to help me make
Naxos safe for colonization."

"Harmall doesn't want to stop you," I told her
weakly.

"I don't know what Harmall wants," she said. "But
I'm not taking anything for granted."

I hesitated before asking, but in the end I just had
to. "What do you think it was that killed your ground
crew?"

"If I knew," she said, "we wouldn't need you, would
we?"

"And just suppose," I went on carefully, "that whatever it was, it can't be beaten. Suppose it makes Naxos
forever uninhabitable by men?"

"If that really were the case," she said levelly, "then
the *Ariadne* wouldn't have completed her mission.
We've taken three and a half centuries already. Another two or three would be comfortably within our
compass."

She bid me good night, then, but I had a feeling
she'd be asking more questions in time to come. She
was a brave lady, I decided, but just a trifle odd.
Maybe she was entitled to be.

When a woman gets to be four hundred years old,
she's entitled to worry about her age.

6

The journey through hyperspace, sad to relate, was
boring and uncomfortable. The first day and a half I
was sick, partly because of the zero-*g* but mainly because of the shots they gave me to protect me from the
physiological effects of the zero-*g*. The trip wasn't supposed to take a long time, but in hyperspace you can
never be absolutely certain how long it *is* going to take,
and it would have been a pity to have to go down to
the surface of a new world with bones that were even a
bit more fragile than usual.

Zero-*g* fills me with a curiously strong sense of
tedium if I have to stay in it too long. I like to float,
and the sensation itself doesn't bother me, but I find it
difficult to *work* in zero-*g*, and it doesn't take me long
to get restless if I've nothing to do with my hands.
Staring at screens isn't really work—not when it's all
that you can do.

The worst thing of all about being on the *Earth
Spirit*, though, was the sleeping accommodation. Only
the captain—not Catherine d'Orsay, the *Earth Spirit*'s
captain—had a cabin to himself. The rest of us were
wedged in three deep on either side of a gangway so
narrow that you had to move along it sideways. For
privacy, there was a thin plastic curtain in the color of
your choice. Mine was black. I didn't like sleeping

46

where other people could hear me. Sometimes I talked in my sleep.

The *Earth Spirit* had a crew of six, not counting its captain, whose name was Alanberg. She wasn't really built to carry six passengers in addition, and our equipment was also putting pressure on such free space as was available. Everybody knew that we just had to put up with it, but no one thought he or she was expected to pretend to like it.

Alanberg did his best to make the run smooth. He invited us one by one to spend a watch in the cockpit, where he explained the instruments and controls to us. When my turn came, I was faintly surprised by the dullness of the account. The screen which reproduced an image of what was supposedly outside was too obviously a computer playing simulation games. All the information was there: the HSBs scattered over the projection for all the world like red-headed pins stuck in a military map.

"What does it really *look* like?" I asked him.

"It doesn't *look* like anything," he answered. "Light does propagate in hyperspace, but haphazardly. It's virtually instantaneous, but it's subject to all kinds of spatial drift. A beam breaks down and scatters very quickly. Seen from here, the *Ariadne* HSB—which isn't, of course, radiating in the visible spectrum at all—looks to the receptors like a sort of misshapen archery target filling half the field. The computer sorts out the photons of the appropriate wavelength and plots the apparent direction of origin, then gradually builds up a scattergram. We simply point at the region of highest destiny and let the warp-field jump us in that direction. Then we replot and jump again. What kind of path we actually follow there's no way of telling, but the optimum is something like three jumps an hour, ship's time. If we take longer jumps we drift too far from the target and in the long run it isn't worth it."

"Is there some kind of limit beyond which you'd find

it impossible to zero in on a beacon, even though you could still pick up its signal?"

"Maybe," he said. "That's one reason for having three beacons around Mars, but we just don't know for sure. Ships that can't get home can't tell us why. We only have information on the runs which work out right. That's what we have to settle for, until someone masters the conceptual geometry in theory well enough to tell us what the hell we're actually doing. All we know at present is that it works—usually."

I'm sure they're working on it," I murmured. It was hard enough on the imagination, no doubt, when they discovered that ordinary spacetime has four dimensions. The extra ones necessary for figuring in hyperspace may not quite defeat our mathematical capabilities, but they do strange things to our three-dimensional habits of thought.

The cockpit, for good reasons, was the least cramped space on the ship, and it was noticeable, once we'd had our little tours, that the man who got invited back (if that's the right phrase) more often than anyone else was the Space Agency man. Maybe he and Alanberg shared a secret passion for word games. Or maybe one another. More likely, Harmall simply played VIP.

The rest of the crew worked in what they called "slots," for very good reasons. Apart from the quartermaster, they were basically machine-watchers and fixers. The quartermaster was a manwatcher (and fixer). It was difficult to talk to them about their work, in the same way that it's always difficult to talk to highly trained specialists, but they were more approachable in connection with their private obsessions. One was crazy about eighteenth century music; one was writing a novel; one was writing a book about the early social evolution of man and the historical break separating hunter-gatherer societies from agricultural societies; one was using spare time on the ship's computers to do fundamental research in artificial intelligence; the last (the quartermaster) was using the rest of the spare time for exercises in computer art. I never did find out what the captain did for laughs. The advantage of all these hobbies, of course, was that none of them took up more space than a couple of bookplates and a bagful of playbeads. The trouble with any kind of biology is that you need organic things (preferably live ones) to work with. There are no amateur naturalists on starships.

Contrary to popular belief, living so close to other people that you're virtually in their pockets is no way to get to know them. When the only privacy available is that attendant upon fulfilling the most basic and vulgar of bodily functions, the ability to be by yourself becomes a valuable commodity. Starship life is the best possible introduction to the art of ignoring people— and to the equally valuable but often underestimated art of being ignored. You become so adept at these fascinating skills that—paradoxically—it's easy to feel threatened by loneliness. All the apparatus of camaraderie which is so easy to maintain when you interact with others only by choice and within delimited periods of time can easily break down, or come to seem utterly hollow and meaningless, when you're within a few meters of five other people for twenty-three hours out of twenty-four. God only knows how rabbits cope.

This is not, of course, to say that meaningful conversations did not take place, or that our transit time to the edge of beyond was fruitless in terms of learning things we needed to know. By playing back databeads supplied by Captain d'Orsay on handheld bookplates we increased our acquaintance with the information her ill-fated groundcrew had actually managed to transmit—food for thought that we desperately needed to nourish our starveling minds.

"Everything," I confided to Zeno and Angelina Hesse, at one of our frequent discussion seminars, "points to one single conclusion. They should *not* have died. The face of their dying sticks out like a sore thumb as the one incoherent circumstance in a compelling and familiar pattern."

(I do not talk like that all the time—only when the mood takes me.)

"It's odd," confessed Angelina.

"It's not possible, I suppose," ventured Zeno, "that they died as a result of equipment failure of some kind. Asphyxiation, perhaps. A purely physical cause seems more likely to me than a biological agent which struck so suddenly and so swiftly."

I would have liked to believe that too, but the last messages transmitted made it absolutely plain that the victims themselves thought that they were under biological attack from within. They spoke of symptoms and signs, and though it was not possible for them to testify as to their actual cause of death—for obvious reasons—the brief commentaries which they gave on the manner of their dying seemed to rule out asphyxiation or conventional poisoning caused by a malfunction in their life-support systems (which, in any case, offered no such testimony of their own).

"Allergy," said Vesenkov, who had not actually been included in the discussion, but who had been listening in. He was a solidly built man, about my height, with steel-rimmed spectacles. His English wasn't as good as it might have been—nowhere near as good as Zeno's—but he exaggerated his lack of capability by choosing to speak mostly in clipped phrases and one-word sentences.

"Could be," conceded Angelina. "But it's not easy to account for the fact that they all developed extreme reactions to the same allergen, let alone the sudden presence of that allergen in their environment. Obviously someone inadvertently carried something from the lab area into the sleeping quarters, but given the sterilization procedures, it's more likely they carried it inside than out. Looks to me like a virus."

"Do you know how difficult it is to get a hookup between an alien virus and human DNA?" I countered. "It's been done, but Scarlatti had to work damned hard to produce the evidence he has, and in no case has the alien virus, even where it's managed to reproduce virions, actually done substantial damage to a host. Viruses don't have much built-in adaptability, and they're just not geared to operating in cells from another life-system."

"The biochemical environment of a human cell isn't too alien from the viewpoint of a virus—even a virus taken out of the ooze of some world where life never got beyond the primeval soup stage," she pointed out.

"Sure," I said. "Biochemical destiny ensures that the replicator molecules which arise in so-called Earthlike environments are always very similar, and the metabolic pathways that build up around them are similar too. Maybe it's wrong to talk of *alien* environments . . . but for a Naxos-built virus to make itself at home in human cells is like a Chinese peasant trying to make himself at home on Sule."

"A virus doesn't have to be 'at home' to kill," she argued. "Quite the reverse, in fact. Most viruses treat their hosts fairly gently. Good tactics. Instant death for hosts is easy extinction for viruses that need to commute endlessly from one host to another. Obviously, what happened to the groundcrew is aberrant, whether you compare it with Earthly viruses infecting Earthly hosts, or Naxos viruses attacking Naxos hosts."

"No virus," put in Vesenkov laconically. "Frog don't catch cold."

What he meant was that viruses tend to be species-specific, or at least limited to a range of similar species. We don't catch diseases from frogs, even within our own life-system.

"I *said* it was aberrant," answered Angelina.

"Aberrant is just a fudge-word," I pointed out. "You're just using it to protect the hypothesis against criticism."

"Food poisoning," said Zeno suddenly. "That would make sense. Not if they were eating out of tubes, the way we do—but they were on the surface, maybe eating from a common pot. Sterile, for sure—but there might have been toxins left over from some previous infection, as in botulism."

"That's easy enough to check," Angelina pointed out. "Did the food come from the same source, and, if so, what was its history?"

"Canaries," put in Vesenkov. "Mice too."

"That's a point," I admitted. "What happened to the animals? Did they die too? And if so, when?"

We thought about that for a minute. Nobody knew. No data. We checked with Catherine d'Orsay, but she didn't know either. She did, however, express the opinion that the food would have come out of individual tubes rather than from some common source, which made twenty simultaneous attacks of food poisoning seem unlikely.

This left us, as you will realize, dramatically short of hypotheses. Aberrant viruses, for all their secondary elaboration, seemed to be left in the lead. Privately, no doubt, we all considered such unlikely outsiders as the possibility that malevolent indigenes had zapped them all with telepathic mind-crunchers, but nobody was going to say a thing like that out loud.

"The more I think about it," I observed, "the more likely it seems that this mysterious killer might sneak up on us, too."

That one buried the conversation. I could have gone on to solicit opinions as to why we'd volunteered to get ourselves into this position, but it seemed pointless. We all knew well enough. It was the age-old dream of the gates of Eden slowly opening wide, with St. Peter standing there to tell us that we'd served out our sentence and cleansed our souls of original sin, and could now come back in. Catherine d'Orsay maybe had it worse than the rest of us, but we all had it—even Vesenkov and Jason Harmall.

We weren't put off by the danger because we knew, after all, that the serpent would still be lurking under the tree of knowledge, and that this time we had to put paid to his little tricks. You can't expect to live in paradise unless you pay the price, now can you?

7

Earth Spirit was a kind of mobile sardine can. *Ariadne*, by contrast, was an ancient castle where no one lived except a handful of tourist guides and a king without a kingdom.

It was old; it was labyrinthine in its complexity; it was a weird place to be. "It," of course, was more properly "she," but I couldn't think of *Ariadne* as a ship. It was a little world.

Castles, of course, are inhabited mostly by the ghosts of the distant past. Their walls and staircases recall the sound of marching men-at-arms, of torchlight and torture, of knighthood and martyrdom. There is a coldness about them. *Ariadne* was inhabited mostly by the ghosts of the future. Its belly was pregnant with a million unborn children; eggs ready to begin division but callously interrupted; empty plastic wombs waiting patiently to be full. And as for coldness . . . there were row upon row of crystal sarcophagi, where you could sleep the dreamless sleep, if you wished, in the certainty of reincarnation; left-handed time machines.

The king without a kingdom?

That was Morten Juhasz, the captain among captains, to whom Catherine d'Orsay had surrendered her short-lived and ill-fated command. He was hawk-faced and firm of countenance, a machine for issuing commands. He was long and lean, and it would have been easy to believe that he had given up taking his shots if it were not for the fact that one could not imagine his bones being brittle.

His attitude to us was ambivalent. He recognized the inescapable logic that led to our being called in, but he resented the necessity. I think he would have liked it better if he could reasonably have given the job to one of his own back-up ground crews. He didn't want outsiders to solve his problems for him. He would have liked it even more if the first crew had succeeded—if Naxos had been as hospitable as, at first glance, it seemed. He knew well enough, though, that if there were authentic experts in alien biology to be used, who could bring to bear years of personal experience and the legacy of centuries of inquiry, then his own people had to step aside.

I was pleased to be assigned a cabin again, if only for a couple of days before we set off on the next stage of the journey (straight down). I felt tired after the long trip on the *Earth Spirit*, where I'd spent a lot of time in my bunk but had slept very badly, almost afraid to dream. To have four walls around me, separating *my space* from the rest of the universe, was a needful luxury. I didn't particularly want to retreat into it, to spend hours glorying in my own company—I just wanted to know that I had it, and that it was there if I needed it.

There was no conducted tour of the *Ariadne*; we

were called instead to a conference with the shipboard's ecosystemic analysts, to make sure that every
idea and item of data had its full exposure. It didn't
solve much: the hypotheses that came out were the
ones we'd already looked at; the new information relating to the nature of Naxos' life-system merely served to
emphasize still further how closely related it was to
Earth or Calicos. There are remarkably few biochemical options open to an evolving water-based life-system, and Naxos had found all the easy answers to all
the difficult problems. The non-conclusion which the
conference reached was that we didn't know, and
weren't likely to find out except by continuing our investigations on the surface.

By the time I retired to my lonely cell, the exhaustion was really eating into my spirit and I was beginning to feel depressed. I knew that I was probably
building up to a nightmare, but the knowledge didn't
help. If anything, it only increased the probability. I
wanted to get to bed, but circumstances conspired to
find delays in the shape of visitors. I wasn't the only
one, it seemed, who was looking for new opportunities
in the luxury of temporary privacy.

The first person to come knocking at my door was
Jason Harmall.

He closed the door behind him, carefully, and
waited for me to invite him to sit down. There was
nowhere to sit except the bed. I took the top end and
let him have the other.

He produced from his pocket a small device that
looked rather like the seed-case of a poppy, broken off
with three inches of stem—except, of course, that it
was made of metal.

"What's that?" I asked, meekly, as he handed it to
me.

"A transmitter," he said. "It won't work directly.
You record a message into it, and then switch func-

tions. It scrambles the message and fires it out as a kind of beep."

"You, I take it, have the receiver to match?"

He nodded.

"I'm not a secret agent," I pointed out.

"I am," he replied evenly.

I looked down at the thing I was holding for a few moments, then said, "Why me?"

"Don't feel privileged," he said. "Dr. Hesse has one too."

"The idea is that anything *I* may find out is privileged information, I suppose? If we figure it out first, we forget to inform Vesenkov."

"I'm not particularly worried about Vesenkov," he said. "I'm not a fool. I know that you'll have to work together, and that you'll be pooling your resources. Vesenkov can be told everything he needs to know— and Zeno too, of course. But Juhasz insists on sending one of his own people down with you—he argued for half a dozen, but I persuaded him that one is enough. It will be Captain d'Orsay, not a scientist. You shouldn't have any trouble keeping *her* on the outside of your investigation. And when you know the answer, you tell *me*, not her—and not Juhasz."

"I don't understand," I said.

"You don't have to."

"I don't *have to* cooperate."

His blue eyes didn't waver. "Dr. Caretta," he said gently, "I presume that you *do* intend to return to the solar system when this is over. You weren't considering staying here forever?"

I thought it over. "All right," I said. "I *do* have to cooperate. But I cooperate better when I understand what I'm doing."

"It's simple enough," he said. "The *Ariadne* mission is . . . out of date. It no longer fits in with our ambitions. Captain d'Orsay, I fear, doesn't quite see things that way. Captain Juhasz even less so. I don't think there's any chance of persuading them to see things our way. Ergo . . . it may be necessary to take independent action. Quietly, of course. Very quietly. There's no need for you to feel any sense of moral dilemma. Your interests lie with ours—indeed, I'd go so far as to say that you *are* one of us."

I was too tired to want to start an argument about us-es and thems, but there was one point that occurred to me as well worth raising.

"They're going to float us down to the surface, aren't they? We're going to ride down in shielded tin cans with chutes."

"That's correct," he said.

"That means we have to get picked up again. I see your point about our being dependent on the *Earth Spirit* to take us home, but we're just as dependent on the *Ariadne* to provide a shuttlecraft that will pick us up. But you want me to hold out against Juhasz if we find out what went wrong with the first crew."

"You have nothing to worry about," he assured me.

"Reassure me," I told him.

"Dr. Caretta," he said, in his nice, soft voice, "if you find out what killed those men—and give us a chance to beat it—you won't have to worry about the possibility of being marooned. We'll be beating a path to your door."

I looked again at the metal toy that was undoubtedly a part of the armory of every well-equipped spy in known space.

I shrugged, and said, "I don't see what I can lose."

He nodded his approval. He was clearly a man who understood the pragmatic point of view. Then he left.

When the second knock sounded I felt a slight surge of desperation. I jumped to the conclusion that it was Catherine d'Orsay, come to keep me from my sleep and to feed my eventual bad dreams with the anxious prospect of being asked to serve as a double agent. Mercifully, I was wrong. It was, instead, Angelina

Hesse, who only wanted to discuss the awkwardness of being a spy for one side.

She showed me her little toy, and I said: "Snap."

"I feel uncomfortably like a cat's paw," she said. Obviously, she'd no more been prepared for this than I had. She'd been plucked from her laboratory in exactly the same way; she'd done far too much good work in biology to have been wasting time spying on the side.

"If we were cat's paws," I pointed out, "we'd have claws."

"Stupidly," she said, "I hadn't quite realized how valuable this planet might be. When the news was broken, I thought of it as a tremendous break—in the context of the study of paratellurian biology. The other implications. . . ."

She let the sentence dangle.

"They wouldn't let d'Orsay communicate with Earth," I said glumly. "She confided in me. *She* hadn't realized what a hot potato it was, either—but I bet she knows now. She went back to the system expecting to find a humanitarian Utopia, cemented together out of three centuries and more of technical and moral progress. I think she was disappointed with what she found."

"How do you think they'll react when they find out that Space Agency wants to abort their program—after three hundred and fifty years?"

"Not pleased. Especially when they're parked on the very doorstep of success."

"They'll go mad," she said. It was possible that she wasn't speaking figuratively.

"What can they do?" I asked. It was meant to be a hypothetical question, accompanied by a shrug of the shoulders, indicating that Juhasz, Catherine d'Orsay *et al* were—like ourselves—merely helpless pawns of a fate they could not control.

"They could switch off the HSB," she replied quietly.

She'd had more time to think since Harmall had had his little confidential chat with her. Now I did some hard thinking of my own—trying to remember just how disillusioned Catherine d'Orsay had been at our little farewell party, and trying to imagine just how Morten Juhasz might have taken the news she'd brought back.

"Do you suppose," I said eventually, "that Harmall might have had the *Earth Spirit* followed?" It had occurred to me that a shipload of soldiers just might come popping out of hyperspace at any moment.

"Maybe," she said.

"This," I opined, "might turn into a real hornet's nest."

She shook her head pensively. "More likely Harmall will want to play it softly. String them along. Let them think our plan and theirs are compatible. He won't spring any traps until he holds all the cards. Our job has to be settled first, before anyone can act."

"By *our* plan, you mean Harmall's. . . . Space Agency's."

"Isn't it ours?"

I wasn't so sure. "If Harmall had come to me back on Sule," I said, "and told me that I'd have to be party to a complicated double-cross, I just *might* have spit in his eye."

"Why do you think he didn't?" she asked, sensibly.

I had to concede the point.

"Anyhow," she went on," do *you* think that the best way to exploit Naxos—given that we're living in 2444 and not 2094—is to let the *Ariadne* zygotes come to term? If this world *is* habitable—and empty of intelligent life—it's one of a kind."

I looked her in the eye. "I don't see why the *Ariadne can't* carry through the original schedule," I said. "Worlds are big places. There's room enough for everyone."

"Space Agency may not think that way."

"I wish I knew which way they *do* think. Come to that, I wish I knew exactly whose vested interests Harmall stands for. Whether you and I are part of 'our' plan or not, I wish I knew who is. Exactly what plan does Harmall want to put in place of the *Ariadne*'s original program? Who does it involve? Are the Soviets in on it? Come to that, is *Earth* in on it? We poor paws don't even know for sure who's riding the cat. The more I think about this business, the less I like it. If they *did* close down the HSB. . . ."

"The *Earth Spirit* could still find her way home," she pointed out.

"But if we missed her," I observed, "we'd have missed the last bus."

"What's switched off," she said, "can be switched on again."

"Yeah—but when? The *Ariadne*'s program is rather long-term. If Juhasz wants to get it well and truly off the ground without the possibility of interference, he'll need years. Twenty, maybe thirty. It's all very well becoming the galaxy's foremost expert on the biology of Naxos, but I don't want to be a pioneer the while."

"You're young enough," she said, with a wry smile.

"You're not exactly old enough to be my mother," I told her.

Silence fell, briefly. She broke it by saying: "We don't appear to have many options, do we?"

"Not really," I confirmed. "We either play along with Harmall, or we don't. There's no possible payoff in the second."

"I suppose that calculating mind is what got you where you are today?" she observed, not without a trace of sarcasm. "And at such a tender age, too."

I wished that she wouldn't keep remarking on my age.

"It pays to be single-minded," I told her. "It's the only way to achieve anything in this world. You must know that—you may have had ten or twelve years' start, but your list of achievements is hardly unimpressive when set beside mine. All my work has been in collaboration—and when you're working on paratellurian biology, collaboration with a paratellurian can give you quite an advantage."

"I meant to ask about that," she said, seeming glad enough of the opening which let her change the course of the conversation. "How did that come about?"

"Pure blind chance," I replied. "Zeno was one of a group of Calicoi students who came to Earth to study. We met at college—I suppose we gravitated together because we were both foreigners. From the point of view of most midwestern Americans, England is at least as far away as Calicos. We shared space in the labs. It just got to be a habit."

"I've worked with Calicoi on Mars," she said. "Not as closely as you with Zeno, of course, but well enough to get to know them . . . if that's possible. Don't you find them a little . . . distant?"

"I daresay they vary as much as we do," I replied. "Zeno's gloomy—he makes a fetish out of finding no joy in the contemplation of Creation—and his lifestyle is somewhat ascetic, but he's not unfriendly. We get along together."

"Maybe you're a little on the gloomy side yourself?"

"I wouldn't say so. Ascetic, perhaps. Maybe distant but not gloomy. Every day in every way life is getting better and better. Maybe. Mother always told me to look on the bright side. I promised her that I would, if I ever found it. A man can't break a promise to his mother, now can he?"

"Was it your mother who told you that you have to be single-minded to achieve anything in this world?"

"It was."

"I thought it might have been. She didn't, by any chance, tell you not to take presents from strange men?"

She held up her little spy device. I reached out to

touch hers with mine, as if we were clinking glasses before drinking a toast.

"Touché," I said.

She laughed, consummating the witty exchange in an
appropriate manner—or perhaps giving it a blessing it
didn't deserve.

"We'd better get some sleep," she said, giving herself
a slight shove that was just sufficient to float her to the
door. "We have a hard day tomorrow."

I watched her go, giving her an ironic salute by way
of signing off.

I fastened the safety-harness around the bunk, making sure that whatever happened during the night, I
wouldn't fly into any metal walls. Dreaming can be
dangerous, in free fall.

8

The next day was strictly business, and consisted almost entirely—at least so far as those of us whose job
it was to solve the mystery were concerned—of exam-
ining data brought back by the various probes sent into
Naxos' atmosphere. There was a good deal of photo-
graphic material relayed up from soft-landed modules,
but it suffered from the age-old handicap. You get a
very narrow view of a single spot, and you know full
well that the local fauna is likely to have taken one

look at the monstrous black metal thing that came whizzing out of nowhere and pulled a disappearing act.

I paid particular attention to the pictures sent back by the probes that landed in the marshland. My reasoning was simple. By all accounts, there was a *lot* of marshland on Naxos. Large masses of dry land were comparatively rare, and oceanic expanses of open water were similarly atypical. Most of the planet's water was spread fairly evenly over the surface. Its marshes were no doubt very various—maybe we'd have to invent fifty new near-synonyms for the word "swamp" even to begin the job of appreciating their subtle variations—but insofar as anything on Naxos was normal, it was some kind of marsh. *Ariadne*'s ground-crew, therefore, had landed somewhere rather exceptional; the fact that they hadn't found very much in the way of animal life wasn't entirely surprising. Charles Darwin didn't find much on his journey into the interior of Patagonia. The real richness of Naxos' life-system would only be revealed by a close inspection of the marshland.

By comparison with Earth, it seemed, Naxos was a real billiard ball of a planet. No great tectonic plates crunching together to raise mountains and produce earthquakes. No vast ranges of volcanic cones. No deep trenches beneath the ocean where the continental masses were literally tearing themselves apart in their ceaseless drift-and-jostle. A placid world, whose waters were hardly stirred by the gentle tidal pull of the little moon. Life here had had it easy by comparison with life on Earth.

What the implications of that fact were, in evolutionary terms, I wasn't entirely certain. The fact that the *Ariadne*'s resources had so far managed to turn up no evidence of any vertebrate creature more "advanced" than a frog didn't for one moment convince me that there *was* no such creature. There was a temptation to embrace the line of argument that because Naxos was a more peaceful world than Earth, natural selection would not have been as powerful an agent of change, and that one would therefore expect its life-system to retain many supposedly primitive features. That could easily give one an excuse for believing that life on Naxos had only just learned to operate on land as well as on water, and that boring, unspecialized amphibians were the order of the day. I didn't like that line of argument much, though, despite its superficial plausibility.

There were two reasons I didn't like it. The first was to do with the assumption that the pace of evolution on Earth had been quickened by the tendency of the surface to undergo constant and sometimes catastrophic change. Evolution may well be the survival of the fittest in the struggle for existence, but that doesn't mean that the harder creatures have to struggle against the vicissitudes of nature the more progress they'll make. Environmental catastrophes aren't necessarily inclined toward eugenics—they're too indiscriminate. One *could* argue that rapid environmental change is bad for evolutionary progress because it causes too many species to become extinct, resulting in frequent massive gene-loss from the system. We tend to assume that what happened on Earth is the "natural progression," especially now we know that what happened on Calicos was virtually a carbon copy. But what about all the other Earthlike worlds, where the hostility of the environment is such that life can only eke out the most miserable of existences, as organic glop, or primeval soup, or whatever you care to call it?

It's arguable that the really *progressive* changes in evolution—toward greater organization and complexity, toward greater individual adaptability and all the range of behavioral abilities up to and including intelligence—come not from the testing of a hostile environment but from *intra*specific competition and selection. My theory, at least, was that the really vital changes in

Earth's evolutionary past happened not as a result of catastrophes and waves of extinction, but during the geologically quiet times, when species had things relatively easy, when mutations weren't penalized so heavily and gene pools could diversify—when there was time, in fact, for nature to conduct her experiments.

On *that* logic, there was no need to expect Naxos to be "primitive" relative to Earth. There was reason enough, no doubt, to expect it to be *different*, but to jump to the conclusion that it was on the same evolutionary path but merely happened to have got stuck at the amphibian "stage" seemed to me to be unjustified. Maybe all life on Naxos—all complex animal life, anyhow—*was* amphibious . . . but if so, I reasoned, it needn't be because there was nothing there more complex than a frog. It might, instead, be because there was so much water on Naxos, so abundantly distributed, that there was no great advantage in *not* being amphibious.

The second reason that I didn't like the evolutionary-arrest hypothesis was the fact that (as far as I could interpret the data) it didn't seem to hold for the plants. *They* weren't stuck in a rut to the extent that they provided a convincing analogue of the vegetation of the Devonian. There were lots of flowering plants, many kinds of trees, and—most significant—lots of different kinds of grass. The insects, too, were very various. Maybe there were no reptiles, which had learned to lay hard-shelled eggs that could survive desiccation. Maybe there were no birds. But to me, that only implied that the complexity of vertebrate life must be expressed some other way. On Earth, the amphibians had been "superseded"; on Naxos they had held their own—maybe by doing things that the amphibians of Earth never had a chance to do.

I nursed these ideas while I looked most carefully at the woefully inadequate information the *Ariadne*'s meager resources had managed to harvest. I didn't voice them too loudly to my companions, though; there were reasons for being discreet. (Reasons, I hasten to add, which had nothing to do with Jason Harmall's passion for secrecy, but with more mundane concerns like the inability to defend my prejudices against skeptical criticism, and the fact that any scientist always wants to have a little theory up his sleeve, in case it helps him to be first to the answer to a puzzle. Intraspecific competition isn't just a feature of gene pools.)

After a couple of hours of studying the photographs and related data I began to feel that the law of diminishing returns was definitely taking its toll, and that there wasn't much more to be learned without actually going into the field. Caution, though, demanded that I soldier on, in case vital clues to the puzzle concerning the deaths of *Ariadne*'s advance guard might somehow turn up. Zeno and Angelina Hesse likewise accepted their burden with good grace. Not so Vesenkov, however, who—as a pathologist—had little or no interest in ecological analysis.

"Time wastes," he pronounced, in his inimitable style. "Plain bloody stupid. Answer in corpses. Rotting away."

He repeated this opinion to Captain d'Orsay, who promised that we would all be under way just as soon as the equipment transferred from the *Earth Spirit* was properly stowed in the capsules we'd be riding down to the surface.

"It's not an easy job," she pointed out. "Falling through atmosphere isn't nearly as smooth as gliding through hyperspace. Even with the best parachutes there's quite a bump when you hit the ground."

"Should use shuttle," growled the Russian.

"Wasteful," she said. "One shuttle would carry ten times as much weight as the four capsules you'll be riding down in. We want the shuttle to drop a whole crew, if there is no danger . . . if you can give us a way to stop what happened once happening again."

"You'd have to use the shuttle anyway, to lift us off," I pointed out.

"If you have proved that there is no danger," replied the captain, "the shuttle which takes down our second crew can bring you back. If you prove that the danger is too great—perhaps there will be no need to bring you back at all."

I could see the economics of the argument, but I didn't have to like it. The simple fact was that using a shuttle which could set us down and then take off again was very much more energy-expensive than dropping us in heat-shielded capsules, but I would have thought that the special circumstances would have permitted a little less parsimony. In the least likely eventuality, we might prove the world uninhabitable and *still* need lifting off . . . and there was also a chance that our survival might depend on the ability to make a quick getaway.

"I heard that Juhasz wanted to send a whole crew down with us," I observed.

"Even had we done so," she replied evenly, "they would have gone down the same way that the first crew went down. We would not have used the shuttle."

To make allowances for her, I guess that spending ten generations and more cooped up in a big tin can with a closed ecology would make one rather oversensitive to questions of energy economics.

"Are you sure that you can put the capsules down on the right spot?" I asked.

She dismissed the question with a wave of her hand. "The computers will calculate the trajectories, and will operate the controls by radio. There will be no problems."

I went back to looking at pictures. Later, we all progressed to endless tables which had been collated out of the biochemical data transmitted back by the research team prior to their demise. Again, there wasn't nearly enough of it to tell us what we needed to know. There may have been clues there, but the possibility of picking them up was minimal. Knowing the composition of alien biomolecules isn't much good unless you also know about their activity and functions.

"Well," I said to Zeno, at the end of it all, "any ideas?"

"Something's missing," he said. "The dry-land ecosystem doesn't make sense. The ground vegetation is waist-high—a tremendous biomass. Nothing eats it except insects. If there are enough insects to crowd out herbivores, what eats the insects? In the marshes, anything might be lurking under the water—but on the land, where do they hide?"

"Perhaps they're just discreet," I said.

He shook his horny head. "There must be more to it than that."

I wasn't so sure. Herbivores don't have to be the size of cows. They might still be under the surface—if one reckoned the level to which the grasses grew as the "surface". They might be any size from fieldmice to pigs. I pointed this out.

"Something," he insisted, "is *missing*. Not from the world, but from this picture of it. There is something the men and the robots alike have failed to see."

"Maybe they're too well camouflaged," I suggested.

"Maybe," he said. I could tell that he wasn't convinced.

We could have continued the discussion for a long time, no doubt, without getting anywhere, but as it happened, we didn't get the chance. We were invited—perhaps summoned would be a better word—to have dinner with Captain Juhasz himself, and we dispersed in order to make ready for the occasion. I took a shower and changed my skinsuit; no doubt if there'd been any way to dress formally for dinner I'd have found it, but shipboard life isn't geared to such intricacies of habit.

He received us in what I supposed to be his cabin.

The bunk was partitioned off, though, and the space we occupied was mostly occupied by a conference table whose screens had been covered with plastic sheets in order to make it resemble a dining table. The chairs had harnesses by which we could secure ourselves but the food was in the same old tubes.

I was faintly surprised to find that neither Harmall nor Alanberg was included in the invitation. Apparently, Juhasz had already spoken to them at great enough length. There were only six at table—the five of us who were scheduled to make the drop and the great man himself.

All through the meal, I was uncomfortable. Juhasz didn't say much while we were actually eating, but he kept looking at us, one by one, and I got the impression that he wasn't much liking what he saw. Indeed, it seemed almost as if he would rather that we didn't exist. I couldn't quite figure that, until he finally opened up and started talking. Then I realized that it hadn't quite been the way Harmall implied, when he had first briefed us on Sule. Juhasz hadn't *decided* to wait for help from Earth at all.

"You may find this difficult to believe," he said, "but we did not expect the *Earth Spirit* to come to us in response to our lighting of the Hyper-Spatial Beacon. We looked upon the lighting of the beacon more as a ritual—hoisting the flag to signal our success. We expected messages of congratulation, perhaps, or silence. It may seem foolish, but we did not expect that we would have made a unique discovery. Indeed, we had anticipated our small and long-delayed triumph as a rather ordinary event. The actual situation regarding the exploration of the galaxy comes as a surprise. Of course, when Captain Alanberg learned of our problem, he was quick to claim that it could be solved more easily with Earth's resources than our own. There seemed to be no way that we could decline his offer of help . . .

but you may understand why I was—and am—a little reluctant to accept it."

He paused, but no one wanted to comment.

"I had not expected that you would bring national boundaries and limited interests with you," he added. "The *Ariadne* came here on behalf of all mankind. It is my opinion that you, too, should be here to work in the best interests of the race as a whole."

He looked first at Vesenkov, and then at me. *How much does he know?* I wondered. *How much has he guessed?*

"The problem," said Angelina calmly, "is to know what those best interests are—or even if it makes sense to talk about the interests of the race as a whole."

"The *Ariadne* and her sister ships were not launched to perpetuate the conflicts that were the sickness of her age," he said, as though it was some kind of explanation. "She was an attempt to transcend that sickness. Captain d'Orsay and I—and Captain Ifere also—were commissioned not just to be masters of a ship, but to be midwives to a new world. *Ariadne* was designed to carry the seed of a Utopia, her landfall was intended to herald the rebirth of mankind—a new and better mankind."

"And when the *Earth Spirit* arrived," I said, "it was as if the past had caught up with you." I said it dryly, trying not to sound contemptuous.

He turned his pale eyes on me, and I had difficulty in meeting his stare. From his point of view, I suppose, I must have seemed the ghost of a distant era, symbolizing many of the sins that Morten Juhasz had tried to leave behind on Earth.

"I want you to understand what you are doing here," he said. "It is important that you do. I do not intend to make Naxos into a second Earth. I will not allow anyone else to make it so."

"Captain Juhasz," said Angelina calmly. "I think everyone here would like to share the kind of dream that you've carried with you across three hundred and fifty years and a hundred and fifty light-years. I don't think anyone wants to make Naxos into some kind of suburb of the solar system, where all the faults of Earth's history can be repeated. To some extent, you're preaching to the converted. The thing is, though, that *Ariadne* isn't alone in the universe. Naxos isn't some kind of a test-tube where your worthy triumvirate can conduct its experiment in social engineering. As you've said, this is something in which *all* men have a stake. I'm assuming, of course, that by 'mankind' you do mean 'all men,' and not some imaginary transcendental collective entity."

Again, he chose not to debate the issue on ground of her choosing, but simply started again.

"I am in command here," he said. "Captain d'Orsay and Captain Ifere, naturally, share in the decision-making process, but we are all of one mind. There is no authority here but mine, and while you are involved in this enterprise you must accept that authority and no other. Is that quite clear?"

"As a disinterested observer," interposed Zeno, with well-concealed irony, "may I say that you are being slightly insulting in assuming that any of my companions has interests and ambitions at odds with your own. Their ambition, like yours, is to further the ambitions of humankind. For myself, I have no hesitation in pledging myself to the same end. Men have always respected the rights and ambitions of the Calicoi, and it is the aim of the Calicoi to work in harmonious association with men. Or do you imagine that I am here solely to look after the interests of my own kind, with a view to stealing this new world away from you?"

Juhasz hesitated. I could appreciate his quandary. Maybe he *did* think that Zeno's presence was intended to give the Calicoi some kind of stake in Naxos. Maybe there was even some truth in that opinion. But saying so out loud was something else. As Zeno had pointed out, it was difficult for him to clarify his suspicions at all without sounding "slightly insulting."

"There is no one disputing your authority, captain," said Angelina. It might have rested there, with all bad feeling smoothed over, if it hadn't been for Vesenkov."

"Bloody not so," he said, brusquely. "My authority is Soviet. No other. You want help, I help. Everybody's friend. Nobody's servant."

While Juhasz weighed that up, I did too. In a sudden fit of madness, I decided that diplomacy could go to hell.

"You can count me in there, too," I said. "I don't think you own this world, and if you think you do I think you're harboring a dangerous fantasy. It's not for *you*—not even your little Holy Trinity—to specify the greater good of mankind. Finding out what killed your people down there is one thing—putting myself under your command is another."

I looked across at Angelina, who favored me with the merest shake of her head and a wry smile. Juhasz looked at her too, inviting her to dissent. She didn't. He didn't bother checking with Zeno. Neither Vesenkov nor I had said anything that wasn't obvious, but the delicate issue was whether we could or should have left it unsaid, content to string the captain along. In the end, it was to me that he spoke.

"And your authority, too, is the Soviet?" he asked, with deadly irony.

"Not exactly," I said.

"No," he said, in the voice of one confirming by emphasis an uncomfortable truth. "Your authority is this Space Agency that your Mr. Harmall represents, which seems—if I understand him correctly—to be connected with some numinous alliance of western nations, but also autonomous to some degree."

"What *they* mean by freedom," put in Vesenkov, with an unusual lack of brevity, "is not knowing who bloody orders come from." It might have passed for a tolerably witty comment—on another occasion.

"I work for the Agency," I said. "So does Zeno. Technically, I think, you do too."

That, too, wasn't a particularly clever thing to say. It was a way of interpreting his position vis-a-vis Harmall that he was guaranteed to resist in the strongest possible terms.

"The world from which the *Ariadne* came," he said, "is not your world. To your world, we owe nothing."

All in all, it wasn't a particularly satisfactory meal, from anybody's point of view.

As we left, I said to Vesenkov: "You certainly fouled that one up, didn't you?"

He looked at me in surprise, possibly with resentment, for a moment or two. Then he grinned, deciding to take it as a joke. He patted me on the shoulder, and said: "Must find answer. Bloody quick time. Before shooting starts." Then he laughed again and zoomed off down the corridor, pulling himself hand-over-hand along the guide rail.

9

When I got back to my cabin there was someone waiting outside the door. Obviously, it wasn't enough that they kept interrupting me. Now they were beginning to form queues.

He looked as if he was even younger than me—maybe twenty-two or twenty-three. He was small and wiry, with a kind of hunted expression that fit in very well with the intellectual climate aboard the ship.

"Dr. Caretta?" he queried. "I'm Simon Norton."

I took his extended hand. He wobbled as we shook—he clearly wasn't used to zero *g*.

"I've heard that you're from England," he said. He didn't sound very sure.

"I was born there," I told him. "Sorry about the name—I come from a long line of Italian ice-cream makers. I haven't seen the dark satanic mills for a while, though."

He laughed at that. "I was born in Nottingham," he said. "I haven't been there for a while, either. Seems like only yesterday, though."

I opened the door, and swayed aside to let him pass. He moved awkwardly over to the bedrail, which he caught onto in order to steady himself.

"I'd offer you a drink," I said, "but as you can see, I'm living in somewhat Spartan conditions."

"Aren't we all?" he countered, weakly.

It dawned on me that when he said that it seemed like only yesterday that he'd said good-bye to dear old England he was being rather more literal than I'd realized. Unlike Catherine d'Orsay, who was on the transit duty roster, this fresh-faced youth must have slept through all three hundred and fifty years. His last memory must be the shuttle journey up from Earth. That was some blackout.

"How was England?" I asked conversationally. I eased myself onto the top end of the bed, looping a safety strap around my ankle to steady myself.

"In a bad way, mostly," he said. "Except Oxford—and presumably Cambridge too. They run the clocks two hundred years slow there."

"What did you study?" I asked.

"Genetics."

I raised an eyebrow. "That's one thing I was wondering," I admitted. "Where are the legions of deep-frozen scientists, eager to catch up on the centuries of material progress? Are you the whole delegation?"

"I'm not supposed to be here," he admitted.

"Oh," I said. "Why not?"

"Orders."

"Why?"

"I guess they thought that you'd be too busy. They wouldn't want us to waste your time. But. . . ."

"But?" I prompted.

He ducked his head to cover a rueful smile. "I wanted to know the answer to the central enigma. I guess I should have been a mathematician—then I'd only have had to ask whether Fermat's last theorem had been solved."

I'd no idea whether Fermat's last theorem had been solved—or, for that matter, what the hell it was. What was slightly more worrying was that I hadn't a clue what the central enigma was either. I told him this, and he looked quite shocked for a moment. Then his face cleared.

"Oh," he said, "of course. Once you cracked the problem, it wouldn't be an enigma anymore. You'll have forgotten it was ever called that."

"Well?" I said, when he hesitated again.

"To us," he said, "it seemed like *the* problem. It had been around for a long, long time—more than a century. I think we should have had the answer, but virtually all funding for two or three generations had been diverted into biotechnics. Commercialization had squeezed out pure research, and theory was in low repute anyway—there was this fashionable argument about the end of theory . . . because we were supposed already to have induced most of what could be induced with the aid of human senses. . . ."

"I know the one," I told him dryly.

"The thing is," he went on, "that we had no real connection between biochemical genetics and anatomy. As far as we knew—and had known for more than a hundred years—the genes in the nucleus were just blueprints for proteins: a chemical factory. We knew that changes in the gene deployment affected gross structures, but we had no idea how. In the nineteen sixties it must have seemed that making the connection between micro- and macro-genetics was just around the corner, but we never got round that corner. The gap in evolutionary theory left by that omission was very serious . . . but as I say, everyone seemed to have other fish to fry."

"That's the central enigma?"

He nodded.

"We're even worse off than you were," I told him. "We not only don't know the answer, we've demoted the question. There've been a lot of distractions while you've been away. The collapse of civilization—that kind of thing. *Après vous—le deluge,* in fact. Genetics only began to boom again in my lifetime. Now we have a new context for the whole science, though—it's not just biology anymore, it's paratellurian biology. Instead of one life-system, we have dozens. It gives us the chance to do a lot of data-chasing and cataloguing—with abundant practical justification, of course. No great theorist has yet emerged who'll tie it all in together. Mind you, there are only half a dozen properly equipped laboratories in the system, so it's not entirely surprising. We four knights errant who have come riding to your rescue are members of a very special elite —though I don't think your three captains truly appreciate that fact."

He was looking at me as if I were insane. I don't know why. After all, it was hardly *my* fault.

"In your own day as in mine," I reminded him, "the nations of Earth were grappling with problems far more basic than your central enigma. It may not be nice to think about, but there are as many people on the brink of starvation in 2444 as there were in 2044, and probably as many or more than there were in 1644. In between times—in between 2044 and 2444, that is—things were always worse and never better. We've been in trouble since you left home . . . for God's sake, that's why you left! Technology—especially biotechnology—is and has been a necessity; science is and always has been a luxury. You must understand that."

"But I don't," he complained. "How can you have technology without science? If technology is a necessity, science must be too."

"In a way," I conceded. "But it's a mistake to think that advances in technology are dependent on advances in science. The technologies that transformed the economy of the Middle Ages—water mills, windmills, heavy ploughs and the horse-collar—were none of them dependent upon any advance in scientific theory. The same is true of the machines that made the industrial revolution. Indeed, it was the proliferation of theory that followed technological innovation, not *vice versa*. Biotechnics is basically fancy cookery. Its theoretical base was laid down in the nineteen thirties, but we haven't exhausted it yet and maybe never will. New knowledge might open up new technological horizons, but it isn't *necessary* when you can find adequate practical measures in what you already know."

He shook his head slowly. "So you still have no firm knowledge relating to the inheritance of structure? You still know a great deal about biochemical blueprints and very little about embryological ones?"

I nodded. "Maybe that old argument about the end of theory isn't so stupid," I said.

I wondered how I'd feel if I time-machined into the future and was told by the local cognoscenti that they hadn't made an inch of progress on all the problems that seemed so immediate and so desperate to me. Not terribly surprised, in all likelihood. It's easy to become cynical about progress once you're aware of the extent to which the machine has seized up.

"Then we don't need you," said Simon Norton. "You're no better than us. When we sent for help from Earth . . . we assumed. . . ."

"The thing is," I said, "that you don't know a damn thing about any biology except Earth's. I do. I know the biochemistry and the diversity of a dozen different systems. I work hand-in-glove with a product of one of them. What's down on the surface is as new to me as it is to you, but it's a different kind of newness. For me, it's part of a pattern. For you, it would be the first encounter with the alien. You do see the difference?"

He thought about it for a moment, and then conceded that he did.

"After all," I pointed out, "you didn't actually dedicate your own life to the noble pursuit of a solution to the central enigma, did you? You threw it over for the chance to be midwife to a new world. A mere biotechnician."

He grinned. "It seemed like a good idea at the time," he said.

It wasn't a sour or sarcastic comment, and was probably more a comment on his own personal ambitions than a reflection on the existential role of the *Ariadne* itself, but it suddenly struck me nevertheless that here was an attitude markedly different from that of Captains Juhasz and d'Orsay.

"Why?" I asked quietly.

"It was the big thing going," he said. "A journey to the stars. The romance was the most important thing. The gene bank seemed like a good idea, in view of the way things kept threatening to go completely to hell. And the prospect of finding a new world was. . . ."

"Like finally getting a return ticket to paradise," I finished for him.

"Stupid, really," he said.

"Not so stupid," I told him. "After all, you came home, didn't you. Dead center."

"Except for all those men and women, down there . . . dead."

"Even if it were to be the case that humans can never live down there," I said, "*Ariadne* would still have done a good job. The HSB you've established here is the most important bridgehead we've so far extended toward galactic center. Even if we can't use Naxos, we need her orbit. A string of satellite stations at sixty-degree intervals is something we need almost as much as we need the world itself. It could change the tempo and direction of our so-called conquest of space. Mere biotechnicians would probably be in demand. However lethal Naxos' life-system might be, it will still warrant study."

He didn't seem to think that was a bad idea. There was no paranoid gleam in his eye, no glint of an obsessive desire to be a demigod supervising the advent of humankind in a new Garden of Eden.

I thought of coming right out with it, and telling him

to spread the word that at least one of his captains was off his rocker, but thought better of it.

"I don't think I could go home," he said pensively. The statement seemed like something of a non sequitur, but his expression was eloquent.

"No," I agreed. "You seem to have cut yourself off from home, rather. Your future's here."

After a pause, he asked, "Do you think you can solve the problem—down there?"

"That depends on what kind of a problem it is," I answered. I didn't want to go through the whole rigmarole again, so I left it at that.

"Well," he said, "I wish you the best of luck."

"Luck," I said, "has nothing to do with it." I didn't say it ungraciously: it was just a throwaway line, intended to put the seal on the conversation. I didn't realize, of course, what a damn lie it would turn out to be.

10

There were four capsules in all. One was entirely filled with equipment, while Captain d'Orsay was scheduled to ride down solo, sharing accommodation with more of our precious luggage. Zeno and Vesenkov were appointed traveling companions, and so were Angelina and myself. It never occurred to me at the time to ask who had made these traveling arrangements.

As spaceships go, the capsule which was to carry us down was signally unimpressive. It was basically spherical, but bulged at the waist into a kind of skirt. The base was shielded to protect the interior from the heat of friction, and the rim of the skirt was equipped with small jets for modifying the attitude of the craft. It had no propulsion unit, of course—it was intended only for descending into a gravity-well, which is a kind of flight that offers few problems except those concerned with slowing down.

It was, as is only to be expected, very cramped. Its two seats were very well-padded and the safety harnesses were awesome in their complexity; these two facts taken together suggested that no one was *entirely* confident about the inevitability of a soft landing.

There was, of course, more equipment packed around us. It was all secured and carefully packaged, and it wasn't easy to see what there was.

The launch went smoothly enough, and I wasn't particularly upset by the gradual feeling of unease that crept over me as the minutes ticked by. We would be in free fall for some time, and the long days in zero *g* made that condition seem quite natural. We were both dressed in specially modified sterile suits. Normal sterile suits are glorified plastic bags intended to be worn for a few hours at a stretch. Ours had been designed to be worn routinely for three or four days, and could be maintained for twice as long without actual danger to life. The main modifications, of course, were concerned with waste disposal and the availability of nourishment. We had light backpacks containing a water-recycling plant and food tubes that could be connected to and disconnected from the feed line without having to break the suit's seal. It required the dexterity of a contortionist, but it could be done. I had no doubt that I'd get quite good at it once I got hungry enough. The air inside the suits was under pressure, and the detoxification apparatus was distributed in a peculiar collar-and-breastplate. The plastic was thin enough to talk through, but we had to raise our voices to be heard even at fairly close range. The radio mike in the capsule had to be pressed to the plastic in order to pick up the vibrations direct if we wanted to hold a serious conversation with the *Ariadne*. I assumed that the same would hold true for Harmall's little recorder/transmitter, which I had put in an outside pocket.

We listened to the technician's calm voice as he told Catherine d'Orsay when her chutes were due to open. Minutes later, he passed on the same laconic message to Zeno and Vesenkov. We knew that the lurch that would come when the drogues began to arrest our fall would be the one real stomach-heaving incident, and we were ready to steel ourselves for that when the bad news began to come through.

"Cap four," he said, with painstaking clarity, though he no longer sounded laconic, "you have a malfunction."

I looked sideways at Angelina. She was looking at me, too. I wondered if my complexion was the same awful color hers was. I snatched the mike from its cradle, and said: "What kind of malfunction?"

"You're safe, cap four," said the voice. "The malfunction is an attitude-jet. There is an error in your angle of approach that we cannot correct, but you are in no danger. Please be calm. The chutes will open in ten seconds, and counting."

He didn't mean that *he* was counting. Some silent crystal display in front of him was flickering away the seconds. I counted inside my head, suddenly very fearful that it was all going wrong, and that the chutes weren't going to open. I was wondering how hard we'd crash, and whether or not we might burn up before hitting the ground, and whether the impact would constitute the biggest catastrophe the surface of Naxos had ever suffered, when the lurch came. It should have flooded me with relief, but somehow it failed to do so.

"Chutes are open," reported the technician. "Descent proceeding normally, cap four. Everything is under control."

I looked at Angelina again, and passed the mike over to her in response to a signal.

"This error," she said urgently, "if you can't correct it, what will its effect be?"

"Still calculating," answered the tech. "Please hold. Cap one is now approaching touchdown. Thirty and counting."

Sod cap one, I thought. *What about us?*

"Cap four," said the voice, still enunciating clearly and refusing to give a hint of alarm, "you will miss target and drift. We are trying to calculate the drift. There is no danger—you will soft-land as normal."

"The bastards!" I said. I tried to sit upright, but was restrained by the harness. My voice carried to Angelina, but maybe not to the *Ariadne*. She hadn't depressed the *transmit* button. She lowered the mike in order to look at me.

"Don't you see?" I said.

"No," she replied.

"Malfunction hell!" I spat the words out as though they were some foul-tasting substance. "That bastard Juhasz has sabotaged us!"

The tech told cap two that it was coming in for touchdown, and we heard Captain d'Orsay acknowledge.

"Why?" asked Angelina. She was wide-eyed and didn't want to believe it.

"Because of Harmall's damned transmitters. He *knows*—he's no fool no matter how paranoid he is. We're being sidelined so that Vesenkov and Zeno can have first crack at the evidence. That way Juhasz gets the news before Harmall. Maybe Harmall doesn't get it at all, but it's certain his magic mushrooms won't let him steal a march. Thanks to him, we're out of the action! A hundred and fifty light-years to solve a mystery and they're slamming the door in our bloody faces! The bastards!"

I was too overwrought even to try to snatch the mike back to let them know what I thought. Angelina, always the cautious one, probably wouldn't have let me have it.

"We don't know that," she said. "And even if it's true. . . ." She let the sentence go.

Cap three, containing Zeno and the Russian, was just approaching touchdown. As soon as that was confirmed, Angelina opened our channel again. I had to admire her composure.

"How far from target will we strike?" she asked coolly.

"Not certain," said the technician. "Hold on. We will fix precisely as soon as you are down. The drift is carrying you away to the southwest."

I tried to remember the outlay of the terrain, but couldn't. One direction seemed just as good—or just as bad—as another. I cursed a few times under my breath, hoping that it would make me feel better. Then we got the countdown signal for the landing, and I started ticking off the seconds instead. It was no more productive or useful as an endeavor, but it seemed more appropriate. My mother always told me that cursing was a symptom of a lack of imagination.

My body was feeling very heavy now, and I was dreading the moment of impact, sure that my bones, weakened by zero g, would be certain to give under the strain. I clenched my fists and closed my eyes. . . .

. . . and down we came, roaring and rocking and lurching and swinging.

For a few moments, I couldn't think what was wrong as the capsule heaved and swung. Then I realized.

"We're floating!" I said, too weak to shout it out. "They've dropped us in the bloody sea!"

The roaring died away, to be replaced by a thinner sound like the dancing of fingertips on a metal surface.

"And to make it worse," I added, overcome by a sudden calmness, "it's raining."

"Hello *Ariadne*," Angelina was saying. "How far from the target are we?"

"We have a precise fix," the technician reported. "You are one hundred and sixty kilometers from target."

I cursed again, demonstrating my lack of imagination. What else was there to do?

"We appear to have landed in water," reported Angelina.

"You've come down in an area we named the everglades," said the technician. "I think the reason will be obvious."

"How far are we from dry land?"

"I take it that you mean continuous land—the kind of terrain where the target area is?"

She really had a firm rein on her temper. All she said was: "That's what I mean."

"About a hundred kilometers," he said. "Perhaps a little more. Actually, though, the more water there is, the easier it's likely to be for you to rejoin your companions. You have a life raft in the capsule. There's a powered glider in cap two, but that wouldn't have been much use to you—it's only a one-man reconnaissance craft."

She glanced sideways at me.

"They packed us a boat," I said. "They even knew where they were going to abandon us."

She shook her head, still unconvinced that we were the victims of a vile plot. She set the mike down, and for fifteen seconds we just listened to the rain. I felt very heavy, and no doubt she did too. Not a bone was broken, but I wondered how I had ever managed to carry such a heavy body through the years of my life.

"Lee," said a new voice. "Are you there, Lee?"

I picked up the mike, and said: "Hello, Zee. I'm here. All in one piece. Is it raining where you are?"

"No," he said. "The sky's clear."

"Some people have all the bad luck."

"Is there anything we can do?"

"I doubt it," I said. "Look at it this way—while you're dissecting rotted corpses in the dome, we'll be down here where the *real* action is, enjoying a vacation."

"It can't be helped," he said.

"Not now it can't," I muttered darkly.

"Sorry," he said. "Didn't catch that."

"Never mind," I said.

The *Ariadne* was waiting to come in again. This, too, was a new voice. I recognized it before its owner identified himself. It was Juhasz.

"Dr. Caretta," he said, "we're all very distressed. I can assure you that the jets were checked before the launch. I can't understand what went wrong, or how."

"These things happen," I said, catching a warning glance from Angelina. "Your technician says that we have a life raft of some kind on board. I hope it has a propeller—I'm not very good at rowing."

"How long will it take you to reach the dome?" he asked.

"A few days," I told him. "Rather too many, in fact. I only hope the dome is safely sterilized by the time we *do* get there. We'll be just about out of food and the recycling apparatus will be reaching the end of its tether. If one of the suits malfunctions, we'll be dead. You do realize that, I suppose?"

If he noticed that I was being aggressive, he didn't show it in his voice.

"You'll have to carry the radio with you," he said. "That way we can continue to fix your position, and can guide you if you lose your way."

"We can trust you to do that properly, I suppose?"

"Of course," he replied.

"Is Harmall there?" I asked.

"He's right beside me."

"Hello, Lee," said Harmall's voice. It sounded quite calm and neutral. "We're sorry about the malfunction. Nobody's fault. I'm sure that you're in no immediate danger."

"Probably not," I said, "but it does hamper the mission somewhat, I fear."

He knew what I meant, but carried on regardless. "It can't be helped," he said. "Do what you can to rejoin the others. In the meantime, I'm sure Zeno and Dr. Vesenkov will do the best they can."

We'll maybe get back in time to bury them if they fail, I said, beneath my breath. It wasn't the kind of comment to consign to the ether.

I put the mike back in its cradle, and turned to Angelina.

"Well," I said, "at least we're here."

11

We'd seen plenty of pictures of variations on the marshland theme, but the camera never does prepare you for the reality. The world has a three-dimensional quality which cameras never capture, and I don't mean that just in the literal sense. When you look at a film you're an outsider looking in; when you're there, the scene surrounds you and engulfs your consciousness.

There seemed to be more color than the pictures had implied. The water surface was covered with flat, rounded leaves whose edges curved over to create a shallow concavity. The leaves were ribbed and veined, and they seemed to extend in groups of three from central stems that also bore cuplike yellow flowers. Colored insects hovered over the flowers in twos and threes, darting back and forth as they ducked briefly into the core from which the languorous petals spread.

The nearest "island" was sixty meters or so away, and consisted of a single vast tree around which was aggregated a trailing skirt of vegetation. It was impossible to say how many individual plants were involved in the mad tangle, but there must have been at least half a hundred different species. Most of the flowers were white and yellow, but there were crimson and purple blooms too. The tree's own blossom was pink. In the distance, similar islands and strands of grass-covered ground gathered to give the illusion that the water was a lake, completely rimmed around.

The sound of insects signaling—a muted chafing and chirring—was audible through the plastic of my suit.

The rain had stopped, but the sky was not yet clear. It looked as if it might start again soon, but the insects seemed to be making the most of their opportunity.

Mercifully, the so-called life raft wasn't an inflatable. When we first found it, our hearts sank; it was a roll of plastic looking for all the world like a carefully stowed shower curtain. Once we released it from the wire mesh that held it in bondage, though, we had the privilege of witnessing one of technology's little miracles. The design of the boat was imprinted in the plastic fiber as a molecular memory, and before our very eyes the orange material unrolled itself, and patiently molded itself into the desired form. It was long, shallow-bottomed and none too wide, but very tough and sturdy considering its weight. In a supplementary kit there were curved rods for supporting a clear plastic cupola over the mid-section. Fore and aft of the cupola, once it was in position, were frames over which we could stretch rubbery membranes, to stop the craft shipping water. The membranes, like the belly of the boat, were colored bright orange. It really was a life raft—the theory was that anyone compelled to use it would be easy to spot once the air-sea rescue organization sprang into action.

Ho ho.

There *was* a propeller. Indeed, there was a whole motor, wired to run off an electrochemical powerpack. Powerpacks we had in plenty, but I still had my doubts about the system. The propeller was intended to run under water, and despite a mesh guard, it looked horribly vulnerable to snagging and snarling in such weed-ridden waters as these. I'd been hoping against hope that we might have gotten a motor with a big propeller to be carried aloft, but the life raft was clearly designed for crashes into Earthlike seas. The best-laid plans of mice and men somehow never seem to connect up right with the jams we get ourselves into. (At least, I assume that the mice don't fare any better than we do.)

The main problem we faced—or, to be strictly accurate, the most problematic decision we had to take—was the question of what to take with us in the boat. We had the duty officer on the *Ariadne* read us an inventory of what we had aboard, and then we began to haggle over it. It was heartbreaking to leave behind items of apparatus transported from Sule by the *Earth Spirit,* but the more complicated items were simply too bulky. Once we had an adequate supply of powerpacks and the materials to replenish our suit supplies there was little enough room left. We had to take the radio, of course. For emergencies we took a couple of paddles, a rifle and a flare-pistol. It didn't seem to me to be enough, but as Angelina pointed out, how many emergencies do you expect to meet in a hundred and some kilometers?

How little she knew.

By the time we had everything ready it was late afternoon. It might have made sense to leave our depar-
ture till morning and spend the night on the padded
seats that would give us a better chance of enjoying a
good night's sleep than we'd be likely to find in the
next week. We were too impatient, though—and we
did want to reach the dome before living inside our
suits became *too* intolerable. We sealed up the capsule
and set sail. We reported this event to Zeno—the *Ariadne* was below the horizon and out of contact.

The boat was better than walking, but it wasn't very
fast, and the course we were obliged to steer was a
very complicated one. There was no hope of sticking
fairly close to a straight line—we were stuck in a labyrinth and the only way to get out was to turn and turn
again, always trying to get a little closer to the
northeast. We took turns at the tiller.

We'd been going about an hour when the propeller
first clogged up with thin green strands of algae. I
knew as I cleaned it that it was going to be a regular
task. How long it would be before the thing gave out
altogether was impossible to guess.

While the boat bobbed silently among the leaf-rafts,
Angelina watched the frogs that moved about on them.
They were mostly fairly small, patterned in bright
colors. Some had pointed snouts with which they
probed the veins and cracks in the leaves. Others had
their eyes set high, like Earthly frogs, so that they
could search for insects and catch them on the wing
with whiplash tongues. I saw one bring down a particularly large fly by spitting at it. I'd seen much bigger
specimens on the islands we passed, but they couldn't
operate out here on the leaf-rafts because they were
too heavy.

"How many different species of frogs can we see
from this one spot?" asked Angelina, as I lowered the

propeller back into the water and secured the motor in its bed with the clamps.

"How the hell should I know?" I retorted. Cleaning propellers is not my idea of a good time.

"Hardly any two are alike," she observed. "Even when the form is similar the colors vary."

"Frogs back home vary their color," I said. "They have all kinds of different patterns, and they change color to camouflage themselves."

"These frogs aren't colored to blend in with the background," she said. "It's more like warning coloration. Though who's being warned off is anyone's guess."

"There's certainly a great deal of variety," I admitted. "But the colors may be significant of courtship displays rather than a warning to predators."

As the boat moved on again, the frogs made themselves scarce, most of them hopping into the water as they saw the orange prow moving toward them. It was sensible behavioral programming—if in doubt, get the hell out.

"You know," said Angelina, "it's rather pleasant here."

With that, of course, it began to rain again.

When darkness fell, we decided to tie up at one of the islands. We picked a large one, which was actually possessed of some solid ground, in the hope of stretching our legs. I tried to guide the boat into a muddy hollow in the shadow of a slanting tree trunk, where there were no matted rafts of vegetation. After a couple of minutes of trying to direct the boat in by means of the tiller, I passed that to Angelina and got one of the paddles, hoping to lever us into position. I wedged it against an overhanging branch, but that just bowed under the force, so I tried pushing it down into the water, knowing that it must be very shallow. That allowed me to maneuver the boat as I wanted, and Angelina moved to secure it. I lifted the paddle clear of the water, and nearly got the fright of my life.

"Jesus Christ!" I yelled, and hurled the paddle from me.

Dangling from the end of it, with its teeth apparently dug right into the plastic, was a thing like a conger eel, its writhing body as long and as thick as my arm. It was thrashing madly, probably none too pleased at being ripped from its muddy haven.

The paddle landed in the water, and temporarily ducked below the surface. When it floated up again, I inspected it carefully to make sure the thing had let it go. Then I plucked it out, and handed it on to Angelina. The teeth marks stood out plainly on the blade. If it had been a leg instead of a paddle, one of us could have stopped worrying about the confinement of a sterile suit, and started worrying about how to get along in life with only one foot.

"It would be a good idea," I said, "not to step in the water."

The rain, was by now no more than a thin drizzle. The sky was leaden gray, without the least sign of the moon or any stars. The twilight was quickly gone, leaving us in Stygian gloom. We did step ashore briefly, but it was too difficult fighting our way through the branches and brambles by torchlight, and we soon returned to the boat, stretching the membranes across the open spaces so that we were more or less sealed in.

I looked around at the clutter, and said, "This is not a good place to sleep."

"Neither is the bare ground," Angelina replied. "At least, we have no reason to think so."

"If Juhasz *did* arrange this," I said, "we sure as hell owe him one."

"He's got troubles enough of his own," she answered. "Even if he did arrange it, write it off as an aberration. Anyone's entitled to be a little unbalanced when they've spent the best years of their life waking up every ten years or so to spend a couple of weeks riding herd on a tin can full of machines. Anyway, I thought you'd approve of him. Your mother would."

. I remembered what I'd said about single-mindedness. As far as forgiveness went, I compromised. I forgave her for the nasty crack, and reserved judgment on Juhasz.

"It's going to be a long night," I said. "Maybe it would be better if we kept going. Even if we only make a few hundred meters, it's that much farther on."

"If we run this boat over a rock," she pointed out, "we're *really* up to here." She put her hand flat beneath her chin. She was right. Hurrying wouldn't help if all we succeeded in doing was killing ourselves a little bit sooner.

I called Zeno to see what was doing where the action was supposed to be.

"We're at the dome," he reported, "but we're not going in tonight. We still have to get the greater part of the equipment over here. For now, we're putting up our own temporary shelter. If it makes you feel any better, it's started to rain."

I reported our situation to the *Ariadne* as soon as she cleared the horizon. They quickly reported back to us on our current position. We hadn't come very far. It was no surprise to hear the news, but I'd been hoping that appearances might have been deceptive.

"You'd better try to sleep," I told Angelina. "I'm going to stay awake for a while. I don't suppose anything can happen, but I'll settle easier if I've watched a couple of empty hours go by.

For a moment, I thought she was going to object, but then she shrugged, and settled back into the space she'd cleared in the bow. I switched off the torch, and sat at the front of the cupola, leaning forward slightly. I couldn't see anything outside, even when my eyes acclimated to the darkness. There was still no starlight to cast even the faintest of shadows.

In conditions like that, one inevitably becomes slowly more sensitive to sounds. The plastic of the suit cut out many slight sounds I'd ordinarily have been able to hear but there were still noises aplenty to catch my attention. There was no croaking of the kind we associate with frogs on Earth. There were whistling noises—sounds that might have come from a high-pitched penny whistle or a flute—but whether they were made by vertebrates or invertebrates I couldn't tell. There were frequent plopping sounds close at hand, which I guessed to be frogs diving from the rafts, but they may equally well have been fish rising to the surface. A couple of times the boat was nudged gently from underneath, and I kept thinking of the awesome teeth possessed by the eel-like thing.

Eventually, I let my thoughts drift off into a long reverie—a tangled web of memories from the recent and distant past that grew gradually more inconsequential. In the grip of the daydreams I must have become drowsy, but I never went to sleep. When the boat lurched, I was instantaneously alert.

Apparently, I wasn't the only one to be surprised, for there was a strange kind of snorting sound from outside. Aiming the torch at the sound, I switched on. The snort had died away to a curious kind of snuffling noise, but now this changed to a yelp.

My eyes were no more ready for the flash than the creature's, but at least I knew what was happening. For him (or maybe her) it was an altogether alien situation. I saw big staring eyes, comical rather than fearsome, and a rounded skull, flattened toward the edge of the snout. The toothy mouth was underneath, but in the instant that I saw it the rubbery lips were puckering over the teeth, and a fraction of a second later something hit the plastic of the cupola with a sharp *splat!*

Then the thing was gone, diving for the muddy darkness.

Angelina, sitting bolt upright, said: "What was it?"

I directed the torch back in her direction, making her cover her eyes with a silver-clad arm.

"I don't know," I said. "It looked like a cross between a plesiosaur and a sea lion, but I only saw the head. I think the body was going to rest in the shallows while the neck explored the foliage. We're probably tied up to its favorite lurk-line. The damn thing tried to spit in my eye, but maybe it was entitled."

"Big?" she queried.

I nodded. "The big ones only come out to play when it's dark," I said. "That's why we never saw them on the film. It had big eyes, though—it doesn't hunt by sense of smell."

She looked out at the pitch-black night, and said: "It must eat a lot of carrots." It was an esoteric reference to some ancient piece of folklore.

"It didn't look *very* dangerous," I said. "A small mouth. One thing does bother me, though."

"What's that?" she asked.

"Spitting is a very peculiar defensive reflex to be equipped with if you spend most of your time lurking underwater. It implies that the fellow he *usually* spits at attacks him on land. He may not be the only monster who rears his ugly head by night."

She considered the thought for a moment, then commented that the sooner we got out of the swamp, the better.

I had to agree.

12

It is, they say, always darkest before the dawn.

This, like most of the things "they" say, is a damn lie. Before dawn, the sky begins to get gradually lighter because of light refracted through the atmosphere. The hours before our first dawn on Naxos were rendered even lighter by the fact that there was a break in the clouds. The rain abated once more, and the stars came out.

The fact that I was awake to see it owes much to the habit of clean living and punctilious routine. I had been so very ready to doze off when night fell because of the marginal desynchronization between the natural event and the artificial day/night cycle aboard the *Earth Spirit*, which I had kept to even on the *Ariadne*. Night, on Naxos, was a fraction over ten Earthly hours long. My habit has always been to sleep for seven. (I could have gotten by on five were it not for the loss of benefit on nightmare nights.) Ergo, I woke up about an hour before dawn, and looked up at the bright stars, whose light was filtered through the raindrop-spattered canopy of the boat's makeshift "cabin."

It seemed the most natural thing in the world to unstrip the seam so that I could see properly.

As I moved, the boat rocked, and Angelina woke up. I could tell that she was on edge by the way she shot into an upright sitting position, her hands reflexively groping for the rifle. She didn't find it. It was laid across my lap.

"What are you doing?" she whispered. At least, it sounded like a whisper—I could barely hear the words and it was inference rather than delicacy of hearing that conveyed their content.

I didn't switch on the flashlight, but laid a hand on her barely visible arm to reassure her.

"Nothing wrong," I said quietly. "Look around. Stay here." I was uncomfortably aware of the fact that I sounded like Vesenkov. She got the message.

After a moment's thought, in which I reflected on matters of practicality and mankind's long-standing but almost-forgotten traditions of gallantry, I passed the rifle back to her, butt first. I picked up the flare pistol instead. It only had two shots in its locker, but rumor has it that really *monstrous* things aren't much intimidated by rifle bullets, whereas a faceful of flaming phosphorus is enough to see off anything up to and including Tyrannosaurus rex.

I was careful not to put my foot in the water as I stepped ashore. There was no sign of my long-necked friend, who would probably have crossed this particular location off his social calendar. I stood in the shadow of the nearest tree, quite still, waiting until I was one hundred percent sure of my poise and alertness. The stars were bright—much brighter than the stars seen from Earth—and testified to the benefits of being part of a relatively dense cluster. The network of branches which extended out from the bole of the tree just above my head cast a curious web of star-shadows on the ground, like a halo surrounding a region of darkness.

After six or seven minutes, I stepped across the web of latticed shadows, and began to move through the thick undergrowth, as quietly as I could.

Something the size of a small pig, bloated and long-legged, squirmed out of my path, heading for the water. I put it down as a big frog, though I couldn't see *that* clearly. Something else squirmed under my foot, and I experienced a momentary vision of teeth sinking into the leathery plastic of the suit's shoe. But the legless thing only wanted to get out of my way.

I tried to tread more carefully, just in case.

In the middle of a patch of open ground, with the vegetation up to my knees, I paused, looking around for a better place to walk. I could see the stems and flower heads moving, stirred by feeding things— guided, no doubt, by sense of smell. In a world of amphibians, I recalled, the sun is an enemy, threatening desiccation. The easy way to cope with it would be simply to avoid it.

In the middle of the open space there was an area of ground where the vegetation was not so coarse and tangled. Indeed, it looked almost flat. I made straight for it, thus demonstrating the perils of overlooking the obvious. I didn't bother to ask myself *why* it looked flat. I got the answer, though, when I reached forward with my right leg to step out on to it, and the foot just kept on going. It wasn't ground at all; it was a pool of water.

I yelped, and tried to draw back, but I was off balance. If the pool had been deep I'd have cartwheeled forward and gone under with all limbs flailing. As it was, my foot hit bottom and I merely batted the raft-concealed surface with my right arm. My left leg came clear of the tangled grass, and in order to stay upright I had to put it down in the water close to its partner.

Then something wound itself around my ankles, tying them together, and I realized that I was in trouble. I tried to break its grip, but I couldn't get my feet to move. Then it began to pull, and I was faced with the undignified prospect of shuffling along in the mud, desperately trying to keep my balance, while it brought me to wherever it wanted me.

I couldn't fire the pistol downward, for fear that it would do far more damage to me than to the beastie, so I pointed at the sky and pressed the trigger. The flare went up as a little yellow spark, then burst into a giant flower of red flames, bathing the whole island with the glow of hellfire.

At least, you would have thought it was hellfire the way the local populace responded. My mind was on other things, and the circumstances weren't right for the taking of a census, but I saw half a dozen hulking things that were a cross between a bullfrog and a turtle squirming over the grass, flattening it as they went with ungainly flipper-feet. I saw something else, too, out of the corner of my eye—something that moved much faster and much more easily. I couldn't even say for sure whether it had two legs or four, but it wasn't squirming—it was *running*. I could hear the splashes as the overlords of this little hunting range returned to their castles beneath the curtain of surface vegetation. Metaphorical castles, of course.

There was nothing metaphorical, though, about the thing which had my feet. Worst of all, it didn't seem impressed by the blaze of red light—from which it was shadowed, of course, by the rafts sitting atop its pool.

Having run out of good ideas of my own, I yelled for help. Angelina appeared at the poolside, rifle at the ready.

I pointed at the surface about a meter in front of me, in the direction that the thing was trying to pull me.

"Put a couple bullets *there*," I said.

She did, and the effect was startling. The grip on my ankles relaxed, and the water was churned up by what seemed to be a dozen thrashing tentacles. I hauled myself clear, and switched on the flashlight, which I still held in my left hand. As the writhing arms cut the floating leaves to pieces, we could see the water growing turbid.

"Dead center," I commented. The operative word, of course, being *dead*.

"Are you coming back now?" she asked, her tone implying that I should never have set out.

"We scientists must not allow ourselves to be intimidated by trivial risks," I told her.

"No," she said, "but are you coming back to the boat?"

"Damn right," I answered. "We'll come back in the morning to see what it was."

By the dawn's early light, we came back to see what there was to see. The pool was still turbid, and colored a most peculiar milky pink. I used the tooth-marked paddle to bring the thing out. It had twelve tentacles, each about one and a half meters long, and a complex body that was very soft and apparently protean.

"Shall we call it a squid or an overgrown sea anemone?" I asked. It was plainly neither.

"These things have red blood, just like you or me," she said contemplatively.

"That's right," I said. "Invertebrates and vertebrates alike. Not hemoglobin, but something like it. Remarkable chemical consistency, if I remember rightly."

She dipped a hand into the milky pink soup. It seemed to have the texture of unset jelly.

"Then what's all this stuff *with* the blood? Fluid protoplasm?"

I didn't know, and turned away in search of anything else of interest that the night's dramatic events might have left behind. I spotted it, about twenty meters away. One of the big bloated creatures that didn't move too well. It was, of course, dead. I went over, wondering whether it had died of shock, or whether it had been caught by some falling part of the expended flare.

As it happened, the cause of death was quite obvious and very much more remarkable. It was stuck to the ground, impaled upon the shaft of a long, thin

piece of cane which certainly hadn't grown up over-
night. I pulled out the shaft, and saw that the business
end, which had been thrust through the frog-thing's
body below the neck, had been shaped to a point.

It wasn't much of a spear, but it was very definitely
a spear. I called Angelina over.

"Look," she said, pointing at the hapless, and somewhat shrunken corpse. "When these things bleed, they
don't just bleed—they leak all over the place." True
enough, beneath the body there was more of the milky
goo.

"Very messy," I agreed. "But what I am holding in
my hands is rather more significant."

She examined the spear, and then looked at me. Her
expression was more eloquent than words could ever
have been.

"Frogmen," she said, with a halfhearted giggle.

"When I fired the flare," I said quietly, "something
ran away. I couldn't see what it was—just the motion.
Nothing like *these* misshapen things." I pointed down
at the murdered creature. It was more toadlike than
turtlelike, but it was obviously not built for jumping.
Its limbs seemed not to have made up their minds
whether to be legs or flippers. They were triple-jointed,
but showed no evidence of boned fingers; they ended in
fleshy fans of tissue. The eyes were small, rounded and
black, and the snout was rounded like a pig's.

"This changes things," Angelina observed.

"Yes," I said. "This changes *everything.*"

We walked slowly back to the boat.

I picked up the radio mike and called to attention
anyone who might be listening. The *Ariadne*'s duty officer acknowledged immediately, but I had to wait for
Zeno. Eventually, he came in.

"This world isn't as primitive as it looks," I said.
"There's evidence here of intelligent life."

"What evidence?" asked the man in orbit.

I told him.

"Hold," he said. "I'm contacting the captain."

"How did he come to leave his supper behind?" asked Zeno, who didn't sound particularly surprised by the unexpected turn of events.

"I frightened him by letting off a flare," I said. "Our arrival here seems to be having a traumatic effect on all and sundry."

"How was the spear sharpened?"

"Nothing complicated," I answered. "It seems to have been honed down by scraping it on a rock. The cane is common enough—it grows in clumps in the mud. It's not what one might describe as high technology. This isn't the kind of terrain where you'd expect the early development of the flint axe."

"Maybe not intelligent at all, then," said Zeno. "Animals use tools."

"Sharpening suggests patience and forethought," I pointed out. It wasn't conclusive, of course. Lots of animals think, after a fashion. Whether or not mice lay plans, dogs do.

"What's this about a spear?" asked a new voice, with more than a hint of aggression. It was Juhasz, of course, and I could tell that he wasn't pleased.

I repeated the story.

"You're lying, Caretta," he said. "This is some kind of trick."

I was genuinely astonished.

"Why would we do that?" I asked.

"You know damn well why," he told me. "You're trying to sabotage this mission."

He's flipped, I thought. *The paranoid streak has really cut loose.*

"Are you sure you've got the right man here?" I asked him. "I'm not much of a mechanic, you know— tampering with attitude jets isn't my line."

"You're crazy, Caretta."

"Now I *know* you have the wrong man," I snapped back.

"There is *nothing*," he said, "in all the data transmitted back by our probes or by our landing party to suggest that there is intelligent life on Naxos. It's impossible! There's nothing more advanced than an amphibian—no reptiles, let alone mammals."

"Well," I said steadily, "there's evidence *now*. And you don't need fur in order to have a brain. The landing party found nothing because they landed in the wrong bloody place. *Here* is where the action is—in the swamps by starlight. And your malfunction dropped us right on the spot. Chance plays little tricks, no?"

"*You're* the one who's playing little tricks!" said Juhasz. "But it won't work. You can't abort the mission *this* way. In fact, you can't abort it at all."

I shook my head wearily, and handed the mike to Angelina.

"Captain Juhasz," she said—sweetly enough, considering the circumstances—"this is Angelina Hesse. The artifact is real. It has clearly been shaped to serve a particular purpose, and used. That signifies intelligence, of a kind. It doesn't mean that we have some alternative human race down here—just that there's something which can think ahead well enough to make a weapon. Until we know more, we can't say much about these creatures. Even birds and monkeys back home on Earth pick up quite complicated tricks and communicate them to one another by example. This may be nothing more. But it's not a hoax, and Lee Caretta and I are not part of some conspiracy against you and your mission. I beg you to believe that."

"I wish I could, Dr. Hesse," said Juhasz. "Indeed, I wish it were so." He said no more.

"Zeno?" she said.

"I heard everything," confirmed Zeno. "What can I say?"

"The only person who's going to convince him is Catherine d'Orsay," she said. "And the only person who seems to be in a position to convince *her* is you. You're the only one who can testify to Lee's reliability."

"I'll try," he promised.

Angelina switched off, and looked at me. I'd taken Harmall's little device out of my pocket, and was contemplating it ruefully.

"It never occurred to me," I said. "I think I loused it up."

"Put it away," she said, tired. "We've got a long way to go."

Every step we took seemed to make it longer and more difficult. More complicated, at any rate.

"And to think," I said, "that Schumann offered me the opportunity to say no. Never for a moment did I contemplate it. Why is it nothing ever turns out the way you expect it to?"

"I don't know," she said grimly.

13

"We're entering the living quarters now," said Zeno. His voice, even over the radio, was crystal clear and as steady as a rock. I didn't make any acknowledgment. He knew that we were listening, and he and Vesenkov didn't need any trivial interruptions. Angelina was busy unclogging the propeller. It was only the first time of that day, and we'd made good headway before it happened.

"Most of the bodies are in sleeping bags," commented Zeno. "One is by the radio. One was trying to get into a sterile suit, but didn't make it. Whatever hit them was fast. The bodies seem well-preserved. No immediately obvious outward signs to offer any clues. I'm putting the set down now—Vesenkov needs my hands. I'll report anything that happens as we go."

I turned away from the radio to look out through the open flap of the cupola, across the carpet of floating leaves.

"Don't let it worry you," I said, "but we're being watched."

Angelina didn't even look up. "Where?" she asked.

"Away to starboard. Twenty meters. A pair of eyes, peeping above the surface." I was looking in another direction now, trying to give no indication that I'd noticed. Her glance was equally casual.

"You're right," she said. "Which one of our nocturnal visitors might it be?"

"The eyes are the right size for the one that spat in my face," I said, "but the position is wrong. Those are carried right on top of the head, just right for peeping."

"You want to take a shot at him?"

"No. Anyhow, it might be a her. D'you think he or she is taking an *intelligent* interest?"

"Can't tell," she said. She turned the propeller experimentally with her finger, then began to set the motor back in operating position. "Shall we head in his direction?" she asked.

"He'd only duck under," I said. "I'd rather see if he follows us. He might even get to like us eventually. Maybe we should throw him something to eat."

"All we've got is some tissue-samples from the dead things on the islet," she observed. "I'd rather not lose them, if you don't mind."

She started the motor, and guided us away in the direction we wanted to go. When I glanced back at the watcher, he'd vanished.

"Can we be out of this watery wilderness by tonight?" I asked her.

"I don't know," she replied. "We can get another fix on our position soon. Are you that keen to start walking?"

I don't like walking much, but I liked wading even less. I said so.

A small creature like a basilisk lizard darted across the leaf-rafts away to port, steadying itself as it ran with a supple horizontally frilled tail. Colored insects settled briefly on the cupola, hitching a free ride for a little way. The sun was shining, but there were big cloudbanks gathering in the west and moving slowly toward us. It was obvious that we weren't going to outrun them, and that we were in for more rain.

Angelina had picked up one of her sealed plastic bags and was looking intently at its contents.

"This milky white stuff that oozes out with the blood," she said. "It's strange."

"It looks like the gel that oozes out of dead slugs in killing solution," I observed.

"That thing you trod on was an invertebrate, wasn't it?" she said.

"That's right."

"But the other was a glorified toad. No relation at all."

"Apparently not."

"Invertebrates use turgor pressure to maintain their shape," she said. "You expect them to ooze. You don't expect the *same* ooze from vertebrates."

"Not much we can do until we have some idea of its biochemistry," I pointed out.

"There's something fundamentally *peculiar* about the animal kingdom in this life system," she opined. I wasn't going to disagree with her.

"Intelligent amphibians aren't impossible," I said. "Look at the fingers of Earthly frogs. It's not difficult to imagine them being modified into hands with opposable thumbs. Some kinds of toad are very good at gripping, in fact. Living mostly underwater, they have the potential to develop big heads, relatively speaking. Looking at it objectively, one might wonder why the frogs didn't make it on Earth. How wasteful to have to invent reptiles and mammals before turning out a really tip-top model. If conditions had been *right* for Earth's amphibians, the way they clearly were *here*. . . .we might be descended from toads ourselves."

"Warts and all," she added.

"Wasn't there some old saw about newts?" I asked her.

"Not that I recall."

"It's a pity we drove all the eccentric ones to extinction," I observed. "It would have been interesting to have seen newts and axolotls in the flesh."

"More eyes," she said. "Starboard again, same distance. Two pairs."

I looked. They were there all right. Not moving. Just watching us chug along past them.

"They're not the spear-users," I said. "They can't be." I didn't like to sound too confident in saying so, though.

"The probes never picked up anything like them," she pointed out.

We both knew that meant nothing. There are a million places on Earth where you could dump a probe which could sit there for years and not catch sight of anything more interesting than a cockroach. You could put one down in the middle of a zoo or a national park and *still* see nothing.

I called *Ariadne* in order to get a new precise fix on our position. The duty officer read the figures back to me, and reassured me that we were getting to the edges of the sticky region and that dry land shouldn't be too far away.

"If I were you, though," he said, "I'd try to find a river. It's all pretty flat, so the waterways are moderately deep and slow-flowing."

"You wouldn't know, I suppose, whether there *is* a handy river?" I asked.

"I don't know that there is," he reported helpfully. "But that doesn't mean to say that there definitely isn't."

I thanked him kindly. As he signed off, another voice chipped in.

"Hello," it said. "This Vesenkov. Was definitely wrong. Not allergy. Is open and shut. Not virus either. Died of poison."

"Poison!" I said. "What kind of poison?"

"One test," he said. "I know, but need proof. Easy. Few minutes. Wait."

I lowered the mike slowly.

"Hold on," the duty officer was saying. "I'll inform Captain Juhasz right away."

Vesenkov wasn't holding, though—he'd already gone.

"Zeno?" I said.

There was no reply.

I was still waiting when Juhasz came in. "What's this about poison?" he wanted to know.

"I don't know," I told him. Then he started asking Zeno and Vesenkov to come in. Nobody took any notice. Vesenkov's few minutes began to drag by.

The propeller caught up in some kind of vine, and the boat began to swing. I hauled it out of the water just as the rain began to fall. By the time I'd untangled it, Vesenkov *still* hadn't reported back. When he did, the best part of an hour had gone by.

"Had to use lab," he said. "Sorry. Two pair hands. Anyway, was right. Poison in water. Drank it with coffee."

"You mean that their water supply became contaminated?" This from Juhasz.

"Yes," replied Vesenkov. "Poison is nerve poison. Like some Earthly snake venom. Also like some Earthly chemical weapon. Quick paralysis. Low dose. No doubt at all."

"How did it happen?" the captain wanted to know.

"Easy," said Vesenkov. "Plain bloody murder."

There was a moment of absolute silence.

"Say that again," I said.

"Is murder," he said. "No doubt at all. One more thing. Nineteen dead."

"So?"

"Ought to be twenty. One gone. No trace."

"Are you telling me," said the captain, slowly, "that one of my crew members murdered the other nineteen, and then left the dome?"

"Is likely hypothesis," said the Russian. There was a charming finality about the way he framed his sentences.

"That doesn't make sense," said Juhasz.

"Poison in water is fact," said Vesenkov. "Supply is sealed and recycled."

"It's impossible," said Juhasz.

"Is bloody obvious," retorted the Russian.

"But *why?*"

"Your problem," replied Vesenkov vindictively. "Not mine. My bit done."

It couldn't have cheered Juhasz up to realize that if what Vesenkov said *was* true, then he didn't need us at all. If there was no fearsomely subtle alien plague, then one of his own people could have cracked the problem easily enough.

Fate seemed to be treating him just as harshly as it was treating us.

But Juhasz was by now well on the way to discovering another point of view.

"In that case," he said, "the world is safe. I could send another crew down tomorrow."

"Wouldn't say so," said Vesenkov, laconically. "People didn't die of disease. Murderer may be sick. How else explain murder?"

I glanced at Angelina. If *that* line of thinking was correct, it might be our problem after all.

"In that case," said the captain, "you'd better find him, hadn't you?"

"Not him," said Vesenkov. "Her. Is needle in haystack. *Your* problem, not mine."

Juhasz switched off in exasperation. I sat back, replacing the mike in its cradle without having uttered a word since my single request for clarification.

"Crazy," I said to Angelina quietly.

"It hadn't occurred to me as the probable outcome," she admitted.

"There isn't any other way the water supply could have been contaminated, is there?"

"Who knows?" she said. "Cheer up. It looks at though there might still be mysteries left for us when we get there."

"Sure," I said. "As long as we don't get murdered in our sleep on the way."

14

With stops and starts and a couple of awkward detours, we didn't manage to reach the edge of the marshland before nightfall, as I'd hoped we might. We decided against any further nocturnal excursions—the clouds, in any case, remained massed above us all night, and the rain never stopped. One of us sat up on guard at all times; I slept first, then took over from Angelina with rifle and flashlight at the ready. The night passed without incident.

We knew that we'd come just about as far as the waterways would take us when the trees began to bunch up and the rather scattered growth of the islets gave way to dense forest. We had to abandon the boat, though, long before we reached what *I'd* call dry land. For several hours we were squelching our way through ponds and reed beds, tiring ourselves out while making all of two kilometers an hours. Even when we were done with the bog, it didn't get much easier. All that happened was that the undergrowth grew lusher and higher, so that instead of wading through water we were wading through matted grass and thorny vines. The only relief we got was in areas where the canopy formed by overlapping trees starved the ground of sunlight, so that we could stride out across a flat bed of humus. Such areas were surprisingly few and far between, considering that the forest seemed so dense. Our average speed increased, but it was obvious that sixty kilometers overland wasn't going to be the nice brisk walk that it sounded. There seemed to be no escaping the fact that just as we'd been two nights in the swamp, so we'd be two nights in the forest. My embittered comment about our suits being just about ready to give up if and when we finally reached the dome seemed less of an exaggeration than when I'd made it.

Zeno, Vesenkov and Catherine d'Orsay seemed to be having a much easier time of it, now they'd got the bodies buried. Zeno gave us a report on how easy it would have been for anyone so inclined to poison the drinking water. The supply tank was beside the inner airlock, and the cover could be removed simply by lifting. It wasn't sabotage-proof because it had never occurred to the designers that anyone would dream of sabotaging it. It wasn't sealed because it was in an area which was itself supposedly sterile and fully protected. All the assassin had had to do was lift the cover momentarily, and tip the stuff in.

The only difficulty was in trying to imagine a reason why anyone would do such a thing. What motive could there possibly be? And what future for the murderer, who had apparently fled the scene of her crime in a sterile suit that would keep her fit and healthy for a couple of days and no more? Even if the environment *was* safe, and she'd shed the suit, what kind of life was she looking forward to, alone in an alien wilderness?

The possible presence on Naxos of intelligent—maybe humanoid—indigenes didn't really add much to the imaginative resources out of which we tried to build an explanation. Unless, of course, you figured that the aliens had obtained some weird kind of control over the girl and *compelled* her to commit the murder; or, alternatively, that it was one of the aliens that had perpetrated the dire deed—either of which notions seemed a little far-fetched.

Inevitably, things got worse. That evening, as Angelina and I were trying to rig up some kind of makeshift tent using the cupola from the lifecraft and the membranes that had covered the fore and aft sections, we were hailed by the *Ariadne*.

"Dr. Caretta," said a voice that I hadn't heard over the link before, though it was one I recognized. "Come in Dr. Caretta." There was something conspiratorial about the tone of the voice.

"I'm here," I said.

"Dr. Caretta, this is Simon Norton. You remember me?"

"I remember."

"I thought you ought to know," he said. "Captain Ifere and some of the officers tried to seize control of the *Earth Spirit* an hour ago. They failed, but Jason Harmall and Captain Alanberg are under restraint aboard the *Ariadne*. The HSB is out. Captain Juhasz thought that ships from Earth were trying to reach us—I don't know whether that's true. Some of our own scientific officers have been confined. I don't know what the captain intends to do. I've got to go now—I only took over while the tech answered the call of nature."

I heard the click of the *transmit* button, before I could thank him. I didn't like to ask if anyone at the dome was listening. If they were, they said nothing.

"Well," I said to Angelina, "where the hell does *that* leave us?"

"It depends on what Juhasz has in mind," she replied reasonably.

"What's in Juhasz's mind," I said, "is a lot of empty space where the marbles once were. All we need now is for *Earth Spirit* and *Ariadne* to start exchanging shots. They could flame down together, leaving us all to play Robinson Crusoe. Then Vesenkov and Captain d'Orsay could shoot it out to decide who gets to be emperor. And the mute HSB that could have been the big stepping stone can wheel around the world forever, waiting until the natives achieve space travel in eighty thousand years or so. Won't *they* be surprised?"

"I take it you aren't going to compete?" she said.

"For what?"

"The job of emperor."

"Hell, no," I said. "I'm not old enough, remember?"

"I don't think we have too much to worry about," she said, after weighing it up. "We don't figure in his grand plans, whatever they finally amount to. I think he'll pass all undesirables back to the *Earth Spirit*. There's no harm in letting us all go home. It'll take three hundred years for anyone to get back here without the kindly guiding light."

"First," I said, "we have to get back to the *Ariadne*."

"I'll lay even money," she offered, "that by the time we reach the dome, the first shuttlecraft will be down. Not that the plague warning is off, Juhasz wants to go right ahead with plan A. That's probably why he fell out with Harmall and precipitated the small war. We'll arrive to find our deportation papers all signed and ready. We'll be missing a great scientific opportunity, of course, and we won't be very popular at home. Bearers of bad news never are. On the other hand, Harmall is the officially designated can-carrier. We played our part, so far as we've been allowed to."

She was a monumental fountainhead of common sense when she was on form. At moments like that she almost reminded me of my mother.

"It would be nice not to have to leave so many loose ends," I observed.

"There are always loose ends," she observed. "We could work here half our lives, and there'd be loose ends all over the place. We could tie up some of the ones we have now, but loose ends are like the Hydra's heads."

"Hercules coped," I pointed out.

"Hercules was a hero. But then," she added with a grin, "Leander was some kind of hero too, wasn't he?"

I grinned back. "Not exactly," I said. "Hero was the other one."

She didn't know what I was talking about. All she knew was that Leander was a Greek name with vaguely classical connection.

"Hero and Leander were lovers," I told her. "She used to put a light in her window at night so he could swim across the Hellespont to meet her. She was a priestess, and the meetings were illicit. He drowned one stormy night, and she cast herself from her window in despair. There are poems about it, but I never looked them up."

"Sweet," she said. "Do you go swimming a lot?"

"About as often as little angels fly."

"I quite like flying," she remarked, subverting the joke. I let it go.

"Speaking of stormy nights," I said, "we'd better finish getting the shelter secured. The rain's getting heavier and the wind is blowing."

We had nothing much in the way of tent-pegs, so we finally decided to secure the canopy by weighting the flaps that once had secured it to the hull of the boat with big, rounded stones. We found half a dozen such stones lurking in the undergrowth; they were hard but not as heavy as they looked. They had the bulk of basketballs, but they weighed less than twenty kilos.

It had rained more or less solidly all day, and the weather showed no sign of improvement. The cycle of evaporation and precipitation seemed to be fairly constant on Naxos. The complex factors which result in such an unfair redistribution of the Earth's watery wealth were mostly inapplicable on Naxos, which looked like the ideal posting for a lazy meteorologist.

As usual, Angelina took the first watch. Once we had established the custom, we didn't like to vary it. Irregular habits, my uncle said (fearlessly facing up to the possibility of self-contradiction), are the bane of a well-ordered life.

It was even more cramped in the "tent" than it had been on the boat, despite the fact that we'd been able to discard several powerpacks before arranging the loads we'd have to carry overland to the dome. There was barely enough room to lie down. Exhaustion, though, is a great sedative, and I soon drifted off to sleep. The dream I was having when I woke up wasn't particularly pleasant, but it was by no means one of my five-star nightmares. It mostly concerned getting wet and trying to attract the attention of passing spaceships with fires that wouldn't produce enough smoke.

The reason I woke up was that Angelina was kicking me, and shouting something about the tent blowing away. I had to get to my feet and help her shift powerpacks outside into the rainstorm in order to anchor the canopy more securely.

We'd just about completed this task when it occurred to me that it shouldn't have been necessary.

"What happened to the goddam stones?" I asked, once we were back inside, dripping liberally all over the groundsheet.

"They went for a walk," she said humorlessly.

"What did they use for legs?" I asked sarcastically.

"It's not a joke," she said, showing the first hint of intolerance I'd seen in her. "They weren't stones—they were animals. They grew heads and legs and they stalked away about their business. They can change shape, and also—it seems—the structure and properties of their tissues. Tortoise-strategy, taken to its logical conclusion."

I began to wish I'd seen it.

"It must have been a shock when you switched on the light," I said.

"Revelation, dear boy. Remember the pink stuff? Liquid protoplasm. The thing which lived in the pool, and the things which came out of the water to feed both had some limited power to modify their form. It's a good trick to be able to turn, if you're an amphibian. As you move from one environment to another, you adapt. It makes so much sense, I wonder the amphibians back on Earth didn't go in for it. Why stick to one metamorphosis when the talent is so useful to retain?"

"They didn't have a chance," I muttered. "Life was too tough for them. They got booted into touch in the evolutionary game. The wrong mutational heritage, and no time to catch up before the violence of the environment shoved them aside. I wonder how they do it?"

"No miracle," she said. "Embryos can do it. It's just a matter of maintaining infantile talents into adulthood, and learning to apply them more widely. Facultative metamorphosis. Must be easy when your soma knows how."

"Axolotls could metamorphose more than once," I recalled. "And they could hold off metamorphosis, too, if they wanted—they could breed as juveniles or adults. I *said* it was a pity we drove them to extinction. Hell!"

"What's up?"

"The indigenes. They might be a race of bloody werewolves."

"Werefrogs," she corrected.

"No," I said, sitting down and trying to think. "It's serious. If this faculty *is* widespread in the life-system—your fundamental peculiarity of the animal kingdom—then the most advanced members are likely to be the ones which use it best."

"Not necessarily," she said. "Intelligence is a different kind of adaptability altogether. You may find that it's the ones who *couldn't* master shape changing that had to invest in cleverness instead. Cows have three stomachs and bats have sonar, but people don't even have claws—their tricks are a different kind."

"But it's different!" I said. "This whole system is different—not a carbon copy of Earth's, the way Calicos is. It *is* possible for evolution to transcend biochemical destiny. We always knew that it was, but until now there was no *instance*. We can't lose this to Juhasz's paranoia. We *can't*."

"You might convince your young friend Norton of that," she said, "but you might still find yourself out-voted—unless you want to stay here under Juhasz's authority."

I shook my head, and then rested it briefly on the palm of my hand.

"Better get back to sleep," she said. "You still have two hours. Tomorrow will be a *hard* day. Save your speculations for the hours when we'll need the distraction."

It was good advice, if only it could be followed. I wasn't up to it. Tired though I was, I couldn't get back to the real state of inertia. I dozed, no doubt, but the slightest sound penetrated to my dream-led thoughts, and when it was my turn to stand guard I was anything but refreshed. Nevertheless, I stood my turn, and though we were not threatened, I would have been ready if we had been. Nothing of any considerable size came near the tent all night, and the only things I shone the light upon were the crazy toadlike creatures I'd taken for stones. Active, they didn't look very different from the creatures on the islet, to which they were no doubt related.

A neat trick, I thought, *to be able to grow legs like that. But can you grow hands that grip? Can you grow eyes in the back of your head? Could you make claws or poisonous fangs? And what do you get up to when it's time for sex?*

In my mind, the possibilities were endless. In the flesh, no doubt, they'd be very much more restricted. In all likelihood, they couldn't do anything more than turn themselves into rocks and back again. What the local masters of the technique might be capable of was something else.

All through the night I was half expecting the trees to take up their roots and march away.

15

Early the next morning, Juhasz called Catherine d'Orsay to inform her that a shuttlecraft was being prepared, and that it would make the drop before nightfall. Looked at objectively, it was hardly an irrevocable move, but in the context of the attitudes prevalent aboard the *Ariadne* it was an unmistakable statement of commitment.

Even Captain d'Orsay asked whether it was wise, and for a few moments, listening in, I wondered whether there was going to be a breakdown in the tripartite accord.

"Captain Juhasz," said Zeno, who took over the position of spokesman from Catherine d'Orsay, "we should point out that the original ground crew never completed their survey. Their untimely deaths may have had nothing to do with the possible inhospitability of the local life-system, but there are no adequate grounds for assuming that Naxos is safe. We really don't know very much about the biology of the world."

"Our original fears regarding the environment of Naxos," replied the captain, "were based on the supposition that alien life might be very different from our own and utterly incompatible with it. Your very existence provides a reassurance that alien biologies are likely to be similar enough to permit humans to thrive on other Earthlike worlds."

"In science," Zeno reminded him, "we do not generalize from such limited data."

I took advantage of the momentary lull which followed that remark to interrupt. "Captain," I said, "this is Lee Caretta. Dr. Hesse and I have evidence that the dissimilarities between the life-systm of Naxos and that of Earth are far greater than the differences between Earth and Calicos. I urge you to wait until we have joined Zeno and Dr. Vesenkov at the dome, and until we have carried out a thorough investigation of the biology of this world. As yet, we are almost totally ignorant."

"Your objections are noted, Dr. Caretta," said Juhasz, "and they are overruled. I have men of my own perfectly capable of carrying out the investigation, and I regret that I can no longer trust your party. When you reach the dome, you may assist my people only until such a time as it becomes convenient to bring you back up to the *Ariadne*. Then, you and your companions will be permitted to leave for Earth."

I felt like yelling at him and telling him what a pigheaded fool he was. In order to help resist the temptation I gave the mike to Angelina and went outside to start packing up the stuff.

"You have all the time in the world, Captain Juhasz," I heard her say. "Your journey has taken more than three hundred years. Five full lifetimes. It would be a pity if it were all to go wrong now because you couldn't contain your impatience."

"Madam," replied the captain, "it is because it has taken us five lifetimes to reach our goal that our patience has worn thin so easily. Had you genuinely come to help us, perhaps things would be different, but you came instead to prevent us from bringing to fulfillment the plan to which we have all devoted our lives. We have no alternative but to exclude you at the earliest possible time from further involvement in our destiny."

She begged him to reconsider. It didn't sound as if it was going to do any good. She didn't bring up the subject of intelligent indigenes. It wouldn't have helped.

She helped me pack up the luggage, and I began to secure her part of the load on her back.

"I'm beginning to ache already," she said.

"The situation is out of hand," I observed. "Juhasz is running on sheer inertia. His discretionary brakes have failed. I only hope that Zeno is busy persuading Catherine d'Orsay that the Holy Trinity would be better off without its godhead."

"Maybe we should work on Harmall," she said. "Persuade him to let Juhasz have things his own way, if only the HSB can be restored. Let Juhasz get his program under way—what will it matter in twenty or thirty years? Which is worth more—the world or the stepping stone?"

"If we knew what Harmall really stood for," I pointed out, "we'd find it a lot easier to deal with that question."

"It might make it easier, too, if we were sure how *we* would deal with the world," she said. "It's all very well to be good ecologists in favor of a policy to let well enough alone—but what kind of politically viable solution would we settle for?"

I had no ready answer to that. I didn't think it was possible to prepare one until we knew all the things that we had to find out about the nature of the life-system and the identity of the creatures who were clever enough to fashion hunting spears out of cane.

We set off on the long walk. Angelina was right; the aching began even as we started out, and things didn't get any easier.

"Think of all those early explorers," I said, when we rested at midday. "They did this sort of thing for fun. Months on end, through trackless jungle far nastier than this, without the benefit of plastic suits to keep malaria out."

"They did have bearers, though," she said, shedding her bundle gratefully.

"One more night," I reminded her. "Definitely the last. Then we can take it easy. Eat, drink and be merry."

"But be careful of the water. Murderers always return to the scene of the crime."

"If they're alive," I added. The thought was too sobering to be amusing.

"Can I have the radio?" she asked.

I unshipped it and handed it over. She started calling the dome, asking for Zeno.

When he answered, she asked: "Have you and Vesenkov completed an analysis of the poison?"

"Certainly," replied Zeno. "Do you want the formula?"

"Not as such. I was wondering about the provenance of the poison. Is it a compound known and used on Earth that might have been brought from the *Ariadne* or easily synthesized? Or does it originate locally?"

"We have considered the point," said Zeno cautiously. "The reason we have not reported is that we are unsure of the answer. The compound is of a kind that was at one time manufactured on Earth—so Vesenkov assures me—for purposes of chemical warfare. Its synthesis would be difficult and hazardous, but we cannot be certain that it has not been derived from some chemically related but innocuous substance within the environment of the dome. With so many plastics around, the amount of organic material available is considerable. On the other hand, the substance is fairly similar to the venom manufactured by some particularly poisonous snakes, both on Earth and on Calicos. It may therefore be of local biological origin."

"If you had to guess," said Angelina, "which way would you go?"

"The second seems to me the more likely," admitted Zeno. "but the possibility that these people had been poisoned once seemed highly *un*likely, and this example continually reminds me to be on guard. It is too easy to reach wrong conclusions from hasty theorizing."

"Thanks," she said. "I'll remember that."

When she signed off, I said: "So what?"

"Have you seen anything equipped with poisonous fangs?"

"That doesn't mean much."

"The animals they examined before being wiped out were mostly little froglike things and insects. I suppose any one of them *might* have been carrying the stuff around in their bodies; and having found it, the missing woman *might* have set it aside without mentioning it, because she intended to use it. But it's all so bizarre!"

"We already know that," I said.

She shook her head. After a pause, I said: "You think the aliens did it, don't you? Not merely werefrogs, but also werepeople. That's a hell of a jump from seeing a few stones grow legs and walk away."

"The missing person had opportunity but no motive," she said quietly. "The natives had motive, but no obvious opportunity. It's all a matter of finding the missing piece."

"Can this really be the fountainhead of common sense I've grown to know?" I asked. "We have a hunting spear and walking stones, plus a little pink ooze and a glimpse of something running. From that, you could reach a million wrong conclusions with the aid of the most mediocre imagination."

"I know that," she said.

"Motives for murder aren't all that difficult to find,"

I said, "if you really believe that murders have to have motives."

"You have to fall back on the logic of insanity," she said. And added: "If that's not a contradiction in terms."

"We're talking about a human being," I reminded her. "What's so out of the ordinary about madness?"

By mutual consent, we let the matter drop. Hasty theorizing—if you could dignify such wild imaginings with the noble title of theory—wasn't going to get us anywhere from our present position. Our big problem was finding the strength to keep walking, not solving the riddle of the universe. The trouble with riddles is that they *may* remain unsolved forever—you have no guarantees. The problem of staying on one's feet and continuing to place one foot in front of the other until one reaches a particular destination is quite a different matter. One way or other, it's bound to be resolved. You do or you don't. My spirits were at a sufficiently low ebb to make me cling to the simpler problem, and even to become quite singleminded about it. There's something comforting about a straightforward matter of either/or.

As it turned out, though, the problem of reaching the dome had angles that I wasn't considering.

You're up to your knees in the water, but the water is black and as thick as oil. It fastens itself around you, gripping and holding you back. The sky is black and the leafless trees are white and brittle, powdery when you touch them. The moon is dead white, too, as it hangs in the sky like a predatory thing, still and silent but always able to change.

There's no sound at all, because your feet won't splash in the water. It parts like treacle as you drag your legs forward. You touch the surface with your fingers and it sticks to them like tar. Black tar and white powder transmute themselves in combination into grey slime.

You have to get to the edge, but you don't know where you are. The moon can't guide you and the only way you have of knowing which way to go is something inside you that drives you on. It's sitting in your head, among the canyons and crevices of your brain, but it carries a cattle-prod that reaches into your guts to sting your heart.

You think your heart may burst and you beg the thing to stop, but it just keeps driving you on, without rhyme or reason or care or compassion or hatred or mother-love.

It will drive you until you drop, or until—what's worse—you burst and spill your blue-black substance into the gloomy waters, where fish will feed until there's nothing left but a brittle husk, powdering in the wind, so the thing in your head can break out of the prison of your skull and grow . . .

and grow. . . .

and grow.

But it's a dream.

Only a dream.

You know that you can't escape, because even if you wake, you have to return. You can sleep forever, but you can only wake for a bare handful of hours. Wakefulness is sleep's concession to the ambitions of the human spirit, and dreaming is proof of their vanity.

You reach your hands out to the moon, and you beg for forgiveness, though you never commited a crime. You'll confess to anything, if only she'll lift you away and let you fly on Angel's wings, high into the sky in search of the stars. You begin to accuse yourself of all the monstrous infamies that you can think of, to show yourself needful of forgiveness. . . .to show that you are so bad that only a saint's love could possibly redeem you . . . but she will not hear. She hangs in heaven like a spider on a thread, turned to stone and wrinkled silver.

You're sinking, and you know it. You're so far away, and getting farther. In the end . . . you'll stop struggling. You'll accept the world of your dreams, which is, after all, the only real world. The other isn't yours . . . it's an alien place, inhabited by demons, but in your dreams, if only you can be forgiven, you can enjoy the darkness and the love . . . all the love . . . more love than the other world contains.

To float is to yield, to sink into the blackness, which no longer seems so viscous, but the heaviness and the cloud of suffocation are growing out of your delirium, spiraling behind your eyes, phosphenes popping like seed pods all around you, and the thing inside your head shaking with silent laughter.

So you beg for mercy and cry for help, and say now that it isn't your fault and that someone else was guilty and that the whole world deserves to suffer if only you can go free because the whole world's to blame and deserves to sicken and die and perish in clouds of flame if one innocent man might be saved to go on all alone, and alone, and alone.

Only the world of dreams is a moral world, and only here can justice be part of your being, a chemical in your blood. Only here can it make sense for all crimes to be rewarded, all suffering redeemed, all guilt cleansed. There's something inside you that doesn't want to run away, that won't let you run away, that always wants to return, that saves you from yourself, that makes you what you are and sucks your blood and caresses your skin and thrusts its stinger into the space behind your eyes.

The trees begin to move and march away, forming ranks and shouldering arms, with flowers falling from the sky and rain like tears that vanishes into mist. All the whiteness in the world is going away, to leave you

beneath the moon, in an infinite sea of blackness, burn-
ing in a sea of tears.

Then the moon goes out, an eye obscured by the lid
of darkness, the lid of the world that seals you in,

forever.

And somehow you're glad that this time it's never to
end ...

. . . .when it does.

So I wake up, cold and wet, and try to wipe away
the sweat with moist fingers, and curse the tangled
blankets that feel for all the world like clinging undergrowth against my skin.

My head is aching, and it's so difficult to feel safe
and reassured, but the light of the sun is already beam-
ing down on me, and I suddenly have the feeling that
it's later than I think.

There's something I've forgotten, and there seems to
be something urgent about the big black gap in my
memory that wasn't there before. I can't remember
where I am or why, and the effort of collecting my
scattered thoughts is making my head split open.

I take myself in hand, and tell myself not to be stupid, that everything will be all right, as long as I take
things calmly, and try not to hurt myself, and make
sure that *nobody knows*. It's all a matter of bluff and
discretion. It really doesn't matter that I've brought
this thing with me, not merely across the solar system
but out into the realm of cold white stars. It really
doesn't matter, because it's still in me, utterly private,
nobody's business but my own, and as long as nobody
knows, it doesn't really exist. It's just me. Nobody else.

And then I remember where I am, and I realize that
something is strange. I put my hand in front of my
face, so I can look at the dew-spattered fingers, and I
make myself feel the cold and the damp all over my
body.

I sit up, and see that I am alone. The wilderness is
all around me. My sterile suit is gone, and with it ev-

erything I was carrying, except for one small thing that is clutched tightly in my left hand. It looks, absurdly, like a seed pod of a poppy when the flowers have fallen away, but it is made of metal.

I cannot help myself.

I curse.

16

"Harmall," I said, "this is Lee Caretta. I'm in trouble. I don't know if you can receive this—or, even if you can, whether you'll be able to do anything about it—but I hope you can. You're the only hope I have. I don't know how this thing you've given me works, but I'm hoping that you'll be able to get a fix on it. I'm not going to move because I don't know which direction the dome is. I may do some shouting, to try to attract attention. Angelina may still be close by. But I won't move. I'll transmit this now, and I'll call again in an hour or so. I'll keep calling, until I'm sure that it's not working. Then I'll think of something else.

"I need help, Harmall. Badly. Get it to me if you can."

I switched off the recorder, and pressed the button that would transmit the message as a scrambled bleep, all the way to the *Ariadne,* if only she was above the horizon. I didn't even know that much. As I'd said, though, I'd keep trying. Getting a signal through was probably my best hope. I didn't want to start walking until I had to. I didn't know how far I might have come from the spot where Angelina and I had set up camp, nor in which direction. The last thing I remembered was anchoring the canopy to protect us from the rain. I had all the hours of darkness and a couple of hours of daylight to account for. Maybe most of the time I had been asleep, but even in my sleep I might have walked.

I'd already tried shouting for Angelina. So far, it hadn't worked. I didn't think it was going to.

I only hoped that I hadn't choked her to death before leaving. I didn't think I had—in none of my previous episodes had anything so gruesome surfaced in retrospective connection with the memory blackout. I had no evidence that I'd ever done anything at all while blacked out—though that, of course, could hardly be taken as conclusive. If I'd been murdering people, though, they'd have caught up with me.

On the other hand, Naxos apparently had a bad track record as far as people's behavior during crazy interludes was concerned.

Previously, I'd always woken up in bed, and that had reassured me. I'd always fallen back into the normal pattern of life, and hence had been able to take it for granted that I'd never left it. This may seem absurd, but I'd never expended any effort trying to discover what had happened during my blackouts. I'd never asked myself why they happened. The only interest in them I had was in trying to avoid anyone else finding out about them. I'd listened for clues to where I might have been or what I might have done, but *not* to answer my own curiosity—more to provide myself with a plausible answer if anyone actually asked. My only interest in the truth, in fact, had been the necessity of finding a convincing alibi.

Now, though, things were different. I hadn't woken

up in bed—I'd woken up in an alien forest, without my sterile suit, barefooted and clad only in a thin one-piece more suited to use as underwear than entire clothing. *This* blackout had taken me from safety and abandoned me in a situation of desperate danger. It was the first time that I had ever thought of the black-outs as *being* dangerous. Always, before, I'd tacitly assumed that they were in some unspecifiable sense benevolent. Problematic, but not hostile. *Now* they were very clearly the enemy.

I took a momentous decision. I didn't want to have any more blackouts. I didn't want to have any more nightmares, either.

Deciding is one thing, though—achieving is another.

I was sitting with my back against the bole of a tree. The ground was covered with soft leaf humus, and was relatively bare. There was a little clearing in front of me, where the spreading branches of three trees inter-wove to screen out the sunlight. Only in the center, where there was a dappled disc of illuminated ground, was there a small clump of ground-hugging flowering plants with crinkly leaves and purple flowers. Their scent was distinct and sweet, eclipsing the other odors of the forest at the point where I had stationed myself.

It was cold in the shadow, but the air temperature was increasing slowly as the sun climbed into the sky. It promised to be a bright day, for once—at least I had not run near-naked into a rainstorm.

I didn't mind sitting still—I was both exhausted and dispirited, and felt no urge to be on my feet and moving. The dome, I knew, was likely to be no more than ten kilometers away, probably in a northeasterly direction, but then ten kilometers might as well be light-years. The ground would cut my feet to ribbons. What would have been, on city streets in stout shoes, a mere stroll taking a couple of hours at the outside, was *here* a very different prospect. I might do it, given time and the determination to cope with pain and laceration, but an error in my bearing of a mere five or ten degrees would send me to either side of the dome, out of eyeshot.

So, at least, the situation seemed. It was a defeatist attitude, no doubt, but there might be time for rallying my shattered courage when I was sure that the message to Harmall wasn't getting through, or was finding no response.

I contemplated the possibility of a cruder signal, and wondered if it really was possible to start a fire by rubbing two sticks together. If the sticks I could find nearby ever dried out, I could try it, but in the meantime the possibility did not look strong.

I wasn't hungry—my stomach, used to the thin but nutritious gruel eked out by the tubes, had long since shrunk, and would not trouble me with alarmist signals. I was, however, a little thirsty—and *that* sensation would not be held at bay by habit. There was moistness everywhere, but I hesitated to gather vegetation in order to wring out a few polluted droplets that might injure me far more than they comforted me. I had an ambivalent attitude to the possibility of alien infection, generated by the custom of taking extreme precautions which never, in actuality, failed. Striking a bargain between thirst and caution was going to be no easy task, and might be a matter of long and careful negotiation.

The feeling that I was being watched crept up on me quite slowly. At first, it was at the very threshold of consciousness—I found myself scanning the hanging curtains of greenery that decked the bushes away to my right with anxious apprehension, and was almost surprised. I put it down to nerves and deliberately looked away in another direction, where there were bare tree trunks and no obvious places to hide; but my eyes were drawn back gradually, until I found myself staring again.

Time went by, though, and nothing happened. When

I judged that an hour or so had passed, I lifted Harmall's device again, and spoke into the mouthpiece for a second time.

"Harmall, this is Lee Caretta. This is a mayday call. I'm in bad trouble. Get a fix on my position if you can, and send someone to help. The quicker they can get here, the better."

I thumbed the *transmit* control, and then froze rigid as something crawled out of the bushes.

It was one of those times when you can hate yourself for being right.

Its gait was froglike, but it hadn't a froglike head. Its forearms were long, and this allowed it to carry its head held high, with its forward-looking staring eyes fixed on my face. Its mouth was lined with sharklike teeth, but it had lips that quivered and puckered as if the mouth were getting ready to spit. I remember the beast in the swamp with the long neck and the startled expression, and the little frogs which could bring down dragonflies with a well-aimed jet of water.

It paused about four meters in front of me, as if waiting to see what I'd do. It was poised to pounce, but somehow I knew that it wasn't about to. I met the stare of its big eyes, and I couldn't doubt that there was a mind behind them.

Two more of the things crawled out of the undergrowth, to take up positions flanking the first.

I slipped Harmall's gadget into my one and only pocket and placed my elbows on my knees, thrusting my hands wide, palm-open. I was trying to look helpless, and I suppose that I succeeded.

Their features began to *flow*. The line of the mouth and the jaw began to change, and their limbs changed, too. They squatted back on their haunches, and then began to stand erect. With the forms they had worn in order to confront me first of all it would have been impossible, but by the time they came to their feet it *was* possible. They ceased to be vicious carnivores, ready to leap upon their prey and rend its flesh, and became humanoid, with smooth skin, able hands and steady eyes.

The middle one puckered his lips, and again I thought he might spit in my eye, but instead he emitted a long sequence of sounds, like notes from a flute punctuated by clicks and pops. No human larynx had a cat in hell's chance of generating patterns of sound like that, and I knew immediately that if we were ever going to talk to these people we'd need synthesizers to help us.

"That's a cute trick," I said, trying to sound friendly. I was referring to the shape-shifting, of course, but it didn't matter a damn. I could have recited poetry or sung rude songs—it would all have been white noise to them.

They weren't even talking to me, it transpired. The speech was an instruction, not an attempt to communicate with me, and what it commanded the kingpin's companions to do, it seemed, was to grab the alien and hold him fast. That's what they did. They took an arm each and yanked me to my feet.

"Take it easy, now," I said, trying to sound as soothing and nice as possible. They were surprisingly strong, considering that they could apparently dissolve and reconstruct their sinews at not much less than a moment's notice.

The leader made some kind of gesture, accompanied by a little click-and-whistle, and my captors encouraged me to move off. Not to put too fine a point on it, in fact, they dragged me.

I tried to indicate by words and gestures that if they wanted me to go with them I was willing and could walk, but they continued dragging me regardless. All attempts to establish some kind of *rapport* came to nothing.

Within minutes, *rapport* and its achievement were no longer the matters foremost in my mind. As I stumbled along between the two who were holding me, taken faster than I cared to go, the coarse grass and the brambles began to tear at my feet, and before we'd gone a couple of hundred meters I knew that my worst fears about the possibility of walking home in bare feet were justified.

Their feet—in fact, their entire legs—were protected by some kind of horny tegument, dark green in color, which contrasted with the silkier texture of the skin covering their upper bodies. Maybe they thought I could grow myself armor just as easily; maybe they just didn't care. They didn't stop, though, and they made no attempt to make things easier.

Within half an hour I was in absolute agony, and the only thought that could stand out against the backcloth of raw pain was the desperate hope that it would end. The only freedom left to me was the decision to try to cooperate, and stay on my feet, or to let go completely and let them drag me. The only difference it made was how much of me—and which particular bits of flesh—were being cut to ribbons.

I had never imagined a first contact between intelligent species taking that form. A touch of aggression, by all means, a trifling misunderstanding with respect to the "take me to your leader" routine, but not the reduction of one partner in the great moment to a gasping, pain-wracked wreck as a consequence of a short walk in the wilderness.

By the time we *did* stop, I'd long since stopped paying much attention to my surroundings. It seemed impossible that I would ever pay much attention to anything else at all, in fact, but when I was finally thrown down on the ground, I was astonished how quickly my scattered wits accumulated. The pain didn't go away, but somehow it grew duller once it was no longer subject to constant renewal. Once the torn flesh was no longer being tortured, it settled down to the routine production of pain, which seemed quite bearable by comparison.

I cleared the tears from my eyes with the sleeve of my one-piece. I dared not look back at my ruined feet, so I looked forward instead.

At first I thought it was evening, but then I realized that we were simply in a gloomy vegetable grotto of some kind. The ground was clear for some thirty meters to either side, and where the branches of the trees did not quite meld together matted rugs of twig-and-vine had been extended between them. There were partitions, too, made out of the same rough "cloth," cutting out squarish shelters and areas of private space. There was no fire, and there were few artifacts, all made of wood. Cups, bowls, spoons, spears.

I looked around uncertainly at the gathering crowd. Their staring eyes were filled with a curiosity that I could recognize all the way across the biological gulf between our species. I was struck by how similar they all were, in this particular guise. There was no evidence of sexual dimorphism, though there were certainly some smaller individuals—presumably children —in the party. There were more than thirty of them, but less than fifty. I didn't take an accurate count.

Standing was out of the question, but I could sit up, supporting myself on one hand, with my injured legs trailing the other way. I did so, trying to get as close as I could to a position of assumed equality. They watched me, as if I were expected to give some kind of performance. They seemed ready to take an interest in whatever came naturally.

Here you are, queer thing—do your bit.

"What do you want?" I asked. My voice was no longer soothing; I couldn't have sounded soothing if I'd wanted to. "I can't do my song and dance act anymore. I can't do magic, and without the right equipment, I can't do miracles. I know I'm supposed to convince you that I'm a god, but for the life of me I can't think how. A cigarette lighter is supposed to be the thing, so that I can introduce you to the miracle of fire, but I don't have one. They went out of fashion, four hundred years ago. All I have is a thing which would look to you like a sculpture of a seed pod. It doesn't do a damn thing."

I paused, and looked around to see what effect the speech was having. They weren't rolling in the aisles, but they weren't throwing rotten vegetables either.

"You're the ones with the canny tricks," I told them. "You do the best froggy carnivore I've seen since the Natural History Museum in London. That one was just a model, though; the real ones became extinct millions of years ago. Only you're not going to become extinct, are you? The amphibians of Naxos have figured out a way to keep on going. Who needs cleidoic eggs when you have the kind of adaptability *you* have, hey? Shapeshifting and intelligence, too—conscious control of bodily form. I bet it took you a long, long time to cultivate *that* little trick. I bet you're clever, too, but you'll never become civilized. You don't need fire to cook your food because you can alter yourselves to digest what the hell you like as easily as you please. You should investigate the wonders of stone, though. It's useful stuff."

They were watching me as if fascinated. I had the crazy idea that I ought to keep talking, in case their fascination gave way to something that would be the worse for me.

"You see in me," I told them, "the very acme of Earth's evolutionary process. A human being, phenomenally intelligent and knowledgeable, able to organize the crossing of the great labyrinth of outer space—not personally, you understand, but I am here as ambassador for the entire race. For myself, I am but a humble toiler in the realm of science—a gleaner in the fields of knowledge, trying to pick up the scraps that my ancestors left behind when they sowed the great harvest of wisdom in the nineteenth and twentieth centuries . . . sorry, I mean *reaped* the great harvest. You'll have to excuse me—I'm not quite up to my best. My feet hurt. I'm not an outstanding specimen of my kind, I suppose, but I am an Englishman, which might mean that I am in some distant sense related to Shakespeare. It's said that if you go far enough back ancestral lines get so tangled up that everybody now alive is related to everyone then famous. England and Shakespeare are, from the viewpoint of aliens a hundred and fifty light years away, of little enough consequence in the cosmic scheme, but he could write speeches better than I can. . . . This royal throne of kings, this sceptred isle. . . .This earth of majesty, this seat of Mars. . . . This other Eden, demi-paradise. . . . This fortress built by Nature for herself. . . . Against infection and the hand of war. . . ."

I found myself laughing, and didn't know why.

This other Eden. . . .demi-paradise. . . .

It suddenly seemed so very amusing. But I wasn't thinking about England. Not any more.

They were tried of my performance now. I could see it in their eyes. They wanted to get on to the next act. I wondered what it was. Then one of them stepped forward from the mass. It may have been the one who first approached me, but I couldn't tell. When I saw what he was carrying, I felt like screaming.

Instead of screaming (which wouldn't have helped) I dragged Harmall's transmitter from my pocket and started yelling into it.

"Harmall! Fix on this and get me the hell *out* of here! The bastard aliens have got me and they're going to kill me. I'll transmit now and start again. I'll keep going as long as I can."

I transmitted the message and opened the channel again. I kept pressing the buttons, one after the other, recording a few seconds of meaningless noise and then transmitting. I wanted the beeps to be flowing into Harmall's receiver, to give him the best possible chance of getting a fix on my position.

If he could.
If he was listening.
If he wasn't, then I was finished.

17

The thing the alien was holding was some kind of switch. Not a light switch. . . .switch as in "long, flexible cane" . . . switch as in riding whip. He didn't look as if he did a lot of riding.

I tried to get to my feet, to move away, but I didn't have a chance and he knew it. The gleam in his eyes no longer signalled curiosity or intelligence, but cruelty. He was going to cut me up and he was going to *enjoy* it.

It got halfway to my feet, and then hurled myself forward, aiming to butt him in the soft white belly. I got a whistle out of him as he failed to dodge quickly enough, but the whole maneuver probably hurt me more than it hurt him. He stuck a knee in my face and I felt the cartilages in my nose grind as blood spouted out.

Then the blows began to fall, and there was nothing I could do but roll up into a ball and try to fend them off as best I could. I tried to take them on my arms, but he was going for any fleshy bit of me he could reach, and he didn't care *what* I did. The damned thing whistled as it cut through the air—a sound that could have been a syllable in their crazy language.

I felt the cloth across my back tearing, and I felt the blood soaking it through.

Now I *was* screaming. It wasn't doing any good, but there was no way I could help it.

My clenched fist, though, was still clicking and clicking at the buttons on the little metal thing, sending forty messages a minute out into the void. All anyone listening would be able to hear in the split-second recordings was a much-interrupted howling. I only hoped that they wouldn't take it for a mechanical fault.

As suddenly as it had begun, it was over. I was sprawled out, face down, still conscious. As before, the moment the torn flesh was no longer being tormented, the pain somehow became *ordinary*. It was well-nigh unbearable, but it was *ordinary*. I could think again—I could even act, if I could find enough strength in my body to lift my head.

I tried, for no better reason than to demonstrate my defiance.

I looked up, at the faces peering down at me, trying to focus on their eyes.

I tried to say something to them.

"You . . ." I began. I was planning to insult them if I could only find the right word. "*You*. . . ."

And then I had to stop, because I saw something that was absolutely beyond belief, so astounding that it *had* to be the product of deranged consciousness. My thoughts froze, and I tried to focus my eyes.

I tried. . . .

and I saw. . . .

and it was *real*!

It was

You! Lying on your back staring up at the pale white ceiling, feeling oh so heavy as if your limbs were made of lead, and you wonder what the problem is and

*why you can't move your eyes at all . . . until suddenly
you realize that you're dead, and you're lying naked in
your coffin.*

*The only lights are six black candles, and you hear
the murmurous voices of the mourners getting closer,
and you know they're coming to see you, to stare and
sneer at you as you lie there past recall. They're
dressed in black, with tall black hats, and their faces
seem long as they float into view from the periphery of
your field of vision. They look down at you like vul-
tures contemplating their next meal, and they mutter
away in such fast, low tones that you can't understand
a word they're saying, except that it's all about you and
it's nothing good.*

*The tears are falling, and you can feel them soaking
into your skin, but you can't tell whether they're real
tears or tears of blood. They ooze into your flesh and
make you feel unclean, making you swell up like a
bloated bladder. . . .rich pickings for the ghouls.*

*You can hear the music now—the missa solemnis
played on a penny whistle, and the faces draw back
as you begin to move on down the aisle of the great
cathedral, whose vaulted ceiling replaces the plain
white one, drawing your gaze higher than you ever
imagined possible and dazzling your sight.*

*You never imagined that you'd be able to eavesdrop
on your funeral, and you feel that you might be guilty
of some especially pernicious voyeurism. You shouldn't
be there, though wherever else you should or might be
is beyond the power of your imagining. Above the
sound of the music and the muttering voices—or perhaps beyond those sounds—there is another noise that
isolates itself and seems louder and softer at the same
time. You can hear it, but you're sure that the congre-
gation can't. It's a sound for your ears only.*

It's the sound of sobbing.

*Someone is crying . . . crying as if the world were
ending, and there's nothing you can do.*

Nothing.

Nothing.

Nothing.

It's not even because you're dead, because being alive wouldn't make the slightest difference. It's a sickness that afflicts the whole world, a plague that rots more than flesh, that eats its way into the heart of everything, a cancer consuming the whole universe, gobbling up the stars.

The funeral seems unnecessary, somehow, as though the world wished you on your way a long, long time before . . . as though you didn't need to die.

The colored light that filters through the cathedral windows is growing dimmer now, as night falls quickly. The voices fade away, and the music reaches its final plaintive phrases before bursting out again, no longer a celebration of human tragedy but a mocking dance which you recognize as the final movement of the Symphonie Fantastique *by Hector Berlioz, which you know so very well, where the demons and spirits enjoy their lunatic dance in celebration of the triumph of evil.*

The ghosts come out of the walls, no longer afraid of the twilight, but there's something pathetic about their capering and you know there's no need to fear them, because you're of their company now and they can't be anything but welcoming anymore. If the devil himself were to greet you, you wouldn't be afraid, because you knew—you always knew—that you belonged to him, and that hellfire would be your just reward. You're filled with a feeling of relief that it's all over. . . .

Except, of course, that it isn't.

There's still the blood. It has to be let out. You know that it's only a simple thing, like the lancing of a boil, but there's something about the idea that makes you cringe and sweat, something that fills you with a terror so limitless it strips you of your intelligence and leaves you whimpering like a puling animal. It has to

*be done, but it's the worst thing in the world, by com-
parison the healing fires of hell are the gentle breath of
the sun.*

*The suffocation is mounting in your throat; your
mouth is full and you're slowly being strangled.*

The blood is coming . . .

is coming . . .

is coming. . . .

And suddenly, insanely, dream is replaced by delirium, and heat is searing my eyelids. I struggle to open
them, and the sky is burning red.

It can't be!

But it can, and it is, and red fire is everywhere, and
instead of the dream carrying me away to hell, wakefulness has brought hell into the world. There is not
only the sight of burning but the sound and the smell.

And the sound, too, of rifle fire.

I realize that the red flame is the flame of phosphorus flares, colored for blood and danger, and that
the rifle fire is scattering the demonic forces, slaying
the vampires and consigning their dust to damnation.

I wish that I could move, but the pain is too much
to bear, and even triumph cannot lift my flesh as it lifts
my spirits. I am not dead, but I am very, very weak.

Nevertheless, I know it as I fall back into the well of
darkness, far from the grasp of wicked dream.

I know it: I am saved.

18

I woke up once more before the reinforcements arrived from the dome, bringing morphia to take away the pain. It was the pain that woke me, I think.

Angelina Hesse was sitting over me, with the flare gun in her left hand and the rifle in her right. It was evening, and the light was fading. She was frightened, knowing that if night fell, they might return.

She saw my eyes open.

"Hello Lee," she said.

"Harmall got my message?" I said.

"He got them. I must have reached the first spot less than an hour after you left it. When they got the second fix . . . I got here as quickly as I could. The party from the dome will be here any minute."

I twisted my neck to look beyond her, at the nearest of the bodies. It was no longer recognizable as something humanoid. The milky pink stuff had oozed out, and the whole form seemed to be half-dissolved.

"It's not pretty," she said.

"I suppose I don't look much better."

"You'll be okay," she told me. "You've lost a lot of blood, and your skin is a mess. They did their best to flay you alive without the benefit of a knife. But you'll live."

There was a moment's silence, and then I whispered: *"Why?"*

"I don't know," she replied, tiredly. "It doesn't make any kind of sense that I can see. Other worlds . . . alien ways. They're preneolithic savages, Lee. We can't expect civilized behavior."

"If Harmall got the message," I said, changing the subject, "does that mean he's no longer a prisoner on the *Ariadne?* Or is the war still going on?"

"I don't know," she said.

"This must change things."

"I don't know," she said again. "Take it easy, Lee. Help will be here in a minute. Let it ride."

The effort of speaking had become too much for me anyhow. I lapsed back into delirious semi-consciousness until the rescue party did arrive, but it was a quiet delirium, washed back and forth by an *ordinary* pain.

Once I was sedated, of course, I lost all track of time, and did not mind it in the least. The dreams which morphine brings are, in my experience, sweeter by far than those which wait in sleep. When I finally did come round again, there was nothing left of the agony but a dull sensation which, though far from comfortable, became unbearable only when I moved.

I was lying on my stomach in a cot, in what I took to be a small sealed-off section of the dome. Angelina—without a sterile suit—was sitting by the bedside, while Zeno, more discreetly packaged, was working with the aid of a small desk computer.

"Are we sterile," I inquired, "or are we not?"

"We're in the lab section of the dome," she told me. My suit was torn while I rushed to your rescue. There seemed little point in resealing it or trading it in for another. Anyhow, you needed a transfusion of whole blood, and I was the right type."

"How am I?" I asked. My voice sounded thick and my tongue was furry. Zeno abandoned his screen and pulled his chair over to the bedside.

"Not so good," said Angelina. "You have a lot of flesh to regenerate. You can do it, but it takes time."

"They beat me up pretty comprehensively, hey?"

"Yes," she said, "they did."

"What's the state of play with Juhasz' Grand Plan?"

"Ticking over," said Zeno. "He's waiting to see if you develop any infections. If you don't, he's going to figure that it's safe."

"He's going ahead, then?"

"It seems that way," said Angelina. "Not that we have access to his most secret thoughts, you understand. The existence of the indigenes doesn't seemed to have changed his mind."

"The HSB?"

"Still out, as far as we know."

Nothing much seemed to have changed.

"Lee," said Zeno softly, "can you tell us what happened? We need to know. It's all rather confused, from our point of view."

I had a drink of water, and then told them what happened—how the aliens first appeared, changed shape, roughed me up as they marched me across country, dumped me on the floor of their rough abode, and finally set out to beat me to death.

"Think carefully," said Zeno. "At the very end— what was going on?"

I thought carefully.

"I was thumbing Harmall's damned transmitter, trying to signal for help. I remember being on the ground, trying to get away from the switch. I remember looking up. I saw . . ."

I'd raised my hand, as if to point at something, and the gesture just froze. My jaw stuck, and I was hung up there, in mid-syllable, for what must have been fully half a minute. I was aware of the fact that they were staring at me, but I just didn't know how to go on.

". . . something," I finished, very weakly. "I can't remember what I saw."

"What about the last message?" asked Zeno, his voice still very gentle.

I tried hard to remember. "I think I said: 'They've got me and they're going to kill me. . . . I'll transmit now and start again. . . . I'll keep going as long as I can.' All you'd have gotten after that would be the much-interrupted sound of screaming."

I didn't like the way they were both looking at me.

"That's not what I mean," said Zeno. But Angelina gestured him into silence, and looked at me even more intensely.

"That's when you blacked out?" she asked, forming the words carefully.

"That's right," I said. "Anything else that came over must have been the sound of them conversing among themselves."

She turned to Zeno and said, "Have you got the tape?"

He moved back to the desk. I watched him as he retrieved a small playback machine from the work surface.

When he sat down again, he turned it on. I heard again the last words I'd spoken—the last words I *remembered* speaking. Then there was the long series of on/off transmissions, with nothing recognizable coming through. That went on for three minutes or so. Then, surprisingly—to me—there was another substantial transmission. It lasted some forty-five seconds. Most of the noises were stuttering, barking sounds that were more like the grunting of a pig than a human voice. It sounded as if someone were trying to form words but choking as he did so, unable to force out more than the odd consonant. In the middle, though, one word formed clearly. It was unmistakably the word "vampire." Then, as the stuttering grew even more desperate, there was a thrice-repeated syllable that I took to be "damn." Finally, the voice trailed off into an eerie screech; the single vowel sound "Eeeeeeeee!"

growing higher in pitch like a feedback scream in a public address system.

Afterward, Zeno switched off the tape.

"That's me?" I asked.

"No one else was there." This observation came from Zeno.

"What does it mean, Lee?" asked Angelina.

I swallowed hard and said, "I don't know."

"When I came into the clearing," said Angelina, levelly, "they were no longer beating you. They were crouching around your body, almost as if they were fighting to get at you. I thought at first that you were dead, and they were fighting for the meat. But it wasn't that—they weren't jackals at a kill. They weren't trying to suck your blood, Lee—they were trying to touch you with their fingers. You lost a lot of blood, Lee—and lumps of flesh, too. Somehow, they ingested most of it, but not through their mouths. But this was later—it must have been fully ten minutes *after* you sent that last message. Do you think that . . . whatever you saw . . . has something to do with that?"

I shook my head, and lowered my eyes. "I don't know," I whispered. "I don't remember."

There was a long pause, while Angelina and Zeno looked at one another to share their puzzlement.

"Look, Lee," she said. "As regards the aliens, Zeno and I think we have it all pieced together. We think we know what happened, but for the moment, it's all speculation. It's an *a priori* argument with no real foundation in what I actually *saw*. I think we might prove it to Juhasz, given time, but it's just possible that you can prove it for us, by giving us the missing piece. We aren't sure, but we think you may have seen something vitally important. I don't want to lean on you too hard when you're in this sort of state, but if we're right, this planet isn't ever going to be colonized—not the way Juhasz wants to do it, and not any way Harmall might want to do it either. It's dangerous in a way that neither of them could have anticipated, and in a way that neither of them will be willing to believe. I don't think we have the time for a slow and steady investigation. I think we may all be in deadly danger. We need you to remember, Lee—and remember spontaneously. It's the only check we can possibly have on our theory."

"I don't know what you're talking about," I told her, "but it's no use. I can't remember."

Angelina turned again to Zeno, and said, "We'll have to tell him."

Zeno shook his horny head, and said, "Not yet."

She thought for a moment, then said, "Okay." She turned back to me. "Why did you go into the forest alone?" she asked. "What happened to your sterile suit? The aliens didn't take it off you, did they?"

I didn't answer.

Eventually, she said: "You can't remember that, either, can you, Lee?"

I rested my head on my forearms, and said, "No."

"What *do* you remember?"

Again, I couldn't find an appropriate answer.

"Do you remember anything that happened after we set up the tent?"

It was out now, and there was nothing that could be done about it. My answer was flat and emotionless. "I don't even remember setting up the tent."

"Have you had other blackouts like that?"

"Not here."

"Elsewhere?"

"Sometimes."

"New year's eve," said Zeno suddenly.

It was only a guess, but I conceded the point. "That was the first in a *long* time," I said. "I never lost so much as a minute since I came to Sule, before then. Nightmares, yes, but no memory loss."

"Nightmares?" echoed Angelina. "Do you have a lot of nightmares?"

"Yes," I said. "Yes, I do."

"Did you have a nightmare the night before you went off on your own?"

"Yes," I said. "And . . . when they were hitting me . . . maybe after they stopped . . . I was hallucinating. I was dead, and listening in at my funeral . . . it started odd, then got crazy."

"Was there a vampire?"

"There's always the vampire," I told her. "But not *that* kind. Suffocating . . . I don't know. Something strange. Inexplicable."

"Did you ever see a psychiatrist about these nightmares?"

"Of course not. Do you think they'd have let me out into space if they'd known—if *anyone* had known?"

"Maybe they'd have been right not to," she suggested.

Curiously, I'd never thought of that before. For the moment, she'd run out of questions. I didn't see where all this was getting us. Apparently, neither did she, because she said as much to Zeno.

"I think we might help him to remember," said Zeno.

I wasn't sure I liked that. I'd known that it was what they were driving at all along, but it seemed more sinister now. As though they wanted to make me remember *everything*.

"Shall I tell you what happened?" asked Angelina. "Before you decided to strike out on your own, I mean." The tone of her voice suggested that it was something *she* didn't particularly want to talk about. By now, though, we were all party to some idiotic tacit conspiracy, and I knew that it would all have to come out. As much of it as *could* come out.

"Go on," I said sullenly.

"I tried to seduce you," she said, and stopped.

"What!"

The exclamation seemed to fall upon the empty air. She didn't respond, though she must have felt that we were both expecting her to. She looked from one to the other of us, and said: "Well, what do you want—a blow by blow account?"

Nobody said a word.

"It's not as if anything much was going to happen," she said. "After all, we were wearing plastic suits, for God's sake! But it was the last chance we were going to have to enjoy any privacy. I wasn't looking for much . . . I just wanted you to—hold me, I suppose. Talk to me. Exchange expressions of devotion. It's not unnatural, you know. Hero and Leander, remember?"

I received this peroration in silence. I still couldn't remember a damn thing.

"And if you say," she began, "that I'm old enough. . . ."

"Shut up!"

We'd been talking very quietly, and the way I yelled then cut across the conversation like a bolt of lightning. But no one seemed to respond. It was as though we'd moved into territory where something like that no longer counted as surprising.

"At the party," said Zeno slowly, "back on Sule. The last time I saw you was when you were talking to a girl—one of the new techs who came in with the Christmas shift. From Astronomy, I think. . . ."

He left the rest to our powers of inference.

"All right," I said, when it didn't look as if anyone else was going to break the silence. "So I don't get along very well with women. It may seem surprising, but that doesn't bother me as much as it should. I'm married to my work, and I don't see anything wrong with that. We live in enlightened times, remember—I'm entitled to run my own life. It doesn't *bother* me."

"Is that why you black out the memories?" asked Angelina. "So that it needn't bother you? Why do you black them out—because they seem to you to be a kind of failure?"

Zeno reached out and caught her arm, and she immediately stopped. "I'm sorry, Lee," she said.

"It's all right," I said. Then, after a moment's hesitation: "It's not as if it's anything that *matters* very much. I don't go berserk when I black out. I don't hurt anyone or damage anything. Why should I be grounded just because I lose a few memories here and there? They're *personal*—they don't affect my work. I'm one of the top men in my field. What could I do if I was grounded? All the vital research in paratellurain stuff is quarantined—the satellite stations, Marsbase. What the hell do you *expect?*"

"Lee," said Angelina, her voice slow with the embarrassment, "I think you should see someone about it. About the nightmares. You really ought to find out why . . ."

"For Christ's sake!" I shouted at her, "I *know* why I have nightmares."

She recoiled from the vehemence of my yell.

"You do?"

"Of course I bloody do. Do you think I'd tolerate having nightmares all my bloody life unless I knew there was a *reason?*"

She turned again to Zeno, and said, "This isn't helping. It's not what *we* need to know."

"Maybe not," said Zeno, softly. "Do you want us to stop, Lee? We don't want to trespass on your private concerns. We thought . . . that you might remember seeing something that would confirm a rather fantastic hypothesis. It doesn't matter that much—and we do seem to have drifted from the point. But if there's any way we can help. . . ."

I tried to raise myself up on my elbows, to get my head as high off the pillow as I could.

"We might as well get it over with," I said, with a sigh. "If I don't tell you, you'll burn with curiosity and you'll never be able to look me in the eye again. We might as well get it all out into the open.

"I've had nightmares ever since I was thirteen. Terrible nightmares—the kind that makes you wake up sweating . . . maybe even screaming. Sometimes, things that happen in my life induce them—sometimes things that happen to me, but more often just things I *hear* about. Things in books . . . newstapes, more often. I suppose that was one reason I had for always wanting to get out into space. Somehow, I thought it would be better, away from *the world,* away from the triggers that set off the dreams. It *was* better, too. Better . . . but they didn't altogether stop. They never will—I know that. Things will still happen to me that remind me . . . and though I can black them out of my memory I can't stop them shaping my dreams. I can't stop the nightmares, because the cause is always there, and always will be there, and nothing will ever knock it out of my memory.

"When I was thirteen, you see, I lived alone with my mother. We didn't have much money. We lived in a two-bedroom flat in a tower block. It wasn't the best area of town. Robbery was endemic—generations of people had lived in the area through centuries of hard times. Maybe a thousand years of the struggle for civilized existence. Generations of buildings, too, bulldozed and rebuilt maybe twice every hundred years, but somehow always the same. The world changed— the Crash had come and gone; before that all kinds of changes going all the way back to the industrial revolution. But one thing had always been the same: people like us were on the fringe, the ragged edge of society. Whatever state the world was in, we were poor. Not starving poor, except during the Crash generations themselves, but *mean* poor and *resentful* poor and *angry* poor. The weak in a strong nation, the non-affluent in an affluent society . . . relatively speaking.

"Anyhow, it was a bad neighborhood. Everybody got robbed once in a lifetime . . . one in thirty was prematurely killed . . . one in two suffered some kind of serious injury inflicted by another. Two men broke in one night, when we were asleep. We had nothing much to steal . . . they looked for something else to make up for their trouble—to make it worth their while. I ran into my mother's bedroom. They followed me from the sitting-room. I tried to yell but one of them put a hand over my mouth, then put a rag into it, and tied a gag so tight I thought I'd choke. Then he tied me to the bedpost—not by my wrists or by my ankles, but with a cord around my neck. My hands were free, but I couldn't untie it, and the more I struggled the more I thought I'd choke. I almost strangled myself, I guess, through sheer terror.

"They raped my mother, one after the other, on the floor. They told her they'd kill me if she wasn't quiet, and she never screamed. She hardly made any sound at all, but she couldn't stop sobbing. All the way through, she just kept sobbing, because she couldn't stop. There was nothing I could do, and nothing anyone could do. They were rough. They forced her . . . well, never mind that.

"They . . . were wearing masks. Stupid masks, made out of cardboard for children to wear. The masks didn't even cover their faces fully—only their eyes and their noses. I don't know how they could see through the eyeholes. But they never took the masks off. Never. They were Dracula masks. Just children's things, trash from some street-market stall or joke shop. Stupid. There was nothing I could do, you see . . . except pull the cord tighter around my throat, until I nearly died.

"After that, I had nightmares. So did she, at first. She outgrew hers, I think—or perhaps she just learned to keep them inside her. When I had mine, then, she'd come into my room and sit on the bed and hold me, but it would take so long for them to go away, and sometimes she'd just start sobbing, and she'd cry as she held me, just the way she had . . . before.

"And since then, you see, I've always had night-mares. Always. Things to do with sex . . . well, they just tend to remind me. That's all. There's nothing more to it than that. Nothing at all."

When I looked up, I saw that Angelina was crying. I couldn't quite understand why.

She looked back at Zeno, and said, "I think we ought to leave it now."

It seemed as if he didn't even hear her. He appeared to be lost in thought. Then his eyes focused, once again, on my face.

"Lee," he said, "what was your mother's name?"

I didn't see the relevance. "*Is,*" I said. "She's alive and well and living in England. Her name is Evelyn. Everyone calls her Eve."

Angelina seemed just as puzzled as I was, but Zeno continued. "Was she less than average height. . . . slightly thin features. . . .with dark hair cut short? Pardon me for saying 'was,' but that *is* what I mean. When she was in her thirties, did she fit that description?"

"Yes," I said, still wondering how and why this qualified as a topic of conversation.

"So was the woman whose body we didn't find," he said quietly. "I think what you saw and what you thought you saw weren't quite the same thing. Your internal censor may have been a little overanxious. I think you *thought* you saw the face of your mother, superimposed on the features of one of the aliens. And I think that what you were trying so hard to say, in that last message which you couldn't remember trying to send, was: 'Adam and Eve.' Could that be right?"

I still couldn't remember a damn thing. Nothing came flooding back into my mind, and there was no moment of therapeutic abreaction. But *another* part of my mind—the calculating part—did react, because I suddenly saw what he was getting at, and realized what his theory regarding the aliens and the murders and the impossibility of colonizing Naxos must be.

"So we stand at the Gates of Eden after all," I whispered, "but we can't pass through."

19

"The trouble is," I said, when we'd talked it through and knew exactly what our theory entailed, "that you won't believe us. Who could we convince, on the kind of evidence *we* have?"

"Vesenkov?" suggested Angelina.

We looked at Zeno, who knew Vesenkov better than we did. He shook his head. "Vesenkov's a pathologist. His imaginative horizons are constrained by the human body and its diseases. In any case, if we could win him with argument and sheer sincerity, it might not do us much good. He's hardly more trustworthy than we are, in the eyes of Captains Juhasz and d'Orsay."

"Did Simon Norton come down with the shuttlecraft?" I asked suddenly. "*He*'ll see the sense of it—he's the only one I know of who's on the right wavelength."

"I don't know," said Angelina. "I don't know what he looks like. I only heard his voice over the radio, and I haven't mentioned it for fear of causing embarrassment."

"Ask," I said. "Find out if he's here, and get a

message to him saying that if he'd like to discuss the central enigma, Lee Caretta would be pleased to have his company for a while."

"What's the central enigma?" she asked.

"He knows," I told her.

When she went out, I let my head drop back onto the pillow, momentarily.

"Are you up to this?" asked Zeno.

"Sure I am," I told him. "I can't get up and dance to take my mind off the pain, but thinking hard works just as well. I just wish that I didn't have this swelling on my nose—it gives me a funny feeling when I breathe. Anyway, if you left me alone to get some deep and healing sleep, I'd probably have bad dreams."

"I'm sorry," he said. "About—all of that."

His clarity of expression was usually much better than that. Long association with humans was obviously leading him into bad habits.

"Do things like that happen on Calicos?" I inquired.

"Where there is intelligence," he said, "there is also evil. Where there is consciousness, there are nightmares. Where there is strength, there is violence."

"Here, too?"

"I am sure of it."

"Hell," I said, "think what nightmares *they* might have."

"They will fear as we fear," he went on, now firmly fixed in his philosophical rut. "Death, dissolution, depersonalization."

"Shapeshifting frogmen are just as vulnerable to *angst* and panic as the rest of us," I mused, refusing to take it quite as seriously as he intended it. "That's good to know. Even though they've invented a new biology, they're stuck with the same old existentialism. Good for God, I say. Original sin is a great leveller."

He didn't say "you should know," which demonstrated his sensitivity to the feelings of others, and proved that he was just a little more discreet than most human beings. Not superhuman, though—not like the Adam and Eve of Naxos.

For the first time (or so it seemed) in a very long time, luck was on our side. Simon Norton *had* come down with the shuttlecraft, and my name—or maybe the mention of the central enigma—was bait enough to make him come along.

"How are you, Dr. Caretta?" he asked, like the well-brought-up boy he undoubtedly was.

"As well as can be expected," I told him. "My name's Lee, by the way. Have a seat."

When he'd sat down he glanced around at Zeno and Angelina, who were so unmistakably *waiting* that he must have known something was up.

"Don't tell me you solved it," he said. "Just by thinking about it."

"No," I said, "I haven't solved it. But I have found the ideal laboratory for studying it. If you want to know about the control of structure, and the heritability of that control, you may learn far more in ten years on Naxos than in a century back on Earth. There's only one problem."

"What's that?" he asked.

"The problem is that the very thing that makes Naxos such an ideal laboratory for that kind of research also makes it an *extremely* dangerous place." I paused, for effect, and then went on: "Naxos is too dangerous even to think of colonizing, Simon. If Juhasz tries to move in here, all his people will be wiped out, and three hundred and fifty years will be thrown away just like *that.*"

I snapped my fingers.

I had tried to sound so confident that I couldn't be disbelieved. I had tried to fill my words with a flat certainty of tone that would permit no disagreement. It worked—almost.

"You'll have to convince me of that," he said.

"I know," I said. "Because after I've convinced you,

you'll have to convince Catherine D'Orsay, who will in turn have to convince Juhasz. If the chain breaks down, people are going to die."

"Go on," he said.

"Do you know what Haeckel's law is?"

"Of course. 'Ontogeny recapitulates phylogeny.' Only it's false, at least in the sense that Haeckel intended it. He thought that embryos *literally* passed through phases representative of the evolutionary ancestry of their species. It's not as simple as that."

"Nevertheless," I said, "the human embryo does at one stage grow structures that resemble gills. There's a sense in which the adult human being doesn't incorporate all the potential contained in its genetic apparatus. By the time the human baby is born, it's pretty much a copy in miniature of what it's going to be when it reaches its final form. The same is true, more or less, of birds and reptiles, and even fish. But the amphibians, which came *between* fish and reptiles, cultivated a different kind of . . . call it 'ontological philosophy.' "

"I know all this, Dr. Caretta."

"I know," I assured him. "But there's an argument in it. The information you have—it's the rhetoric that I'm trying to get across. Bear with me. What do you know about axolotls?"

"They're extinct."

"Apart from that."

"The axolotl was the larval stage of a kind of salamander. But it didn't have to undergo metamorphosis to the adult form before breeding. If its habitat stayed wet enough, it could grow reproductive organs while still a larva, and breed without bothering with the adult form at all."

"That's right. It kept its ontological options open. Now, just suppose that things had been a little different on the ancient Earth. Suppose physical conditions and climate had been much more stable. Suppose water had been much more generously distributed across the surface. Suppose the selective pressure which encouraged the amphibians to develop the cleidoic egg, so that a favored few of their number could become reptiles, wasn't very strong. Suppose the evolutionary story had therefore taken a different tack, investing heavily in the kind of stategies that we can see palely foreshadowed in the axolotl, with the emphasis not only on metamorphosis but on extending the range of possible metamorphoses and the degree of control that an organism's nervous system could exert *over* processes of metamorphosis. Do you see where the argument heads?"

He sighed, and I could tell that he was getting impatient. He wanted to get to the punchline, but I had my reasons for going one step at a time. The speculative part of the argument had to be as nearly seamless as was possible—compelling in its plausibility.

"It leads to a world like Naxos," he said, "where the amphibians never gave way to reptiles, and where the higher animals have several possible forms and can change from one to another as circumstances demand. When they swim, they can shape themselves for swimming; when they walk, they can shape themselves for walking; when they're attacked they can grow some kind of defensive apparatus if they're not taken too much by surprise; when they're asleep they can make themselves well-nigh invulnerable by turning themselves into hard-shelled pseudo-rocks. We've heard from Dr. Hesse about your adventures in the everglades." He paused, and grinned, and then said: "By the way, is it true that you recited John of Gaunt's speech from *Richard III* while the aliens were torturing you?"

"Only a bit of it," I replied dryly. "And it was *before* they started hitting me. Can I get back to the argument?"

He nodded.

"We're about to move beyond the bit that's as easy as ABC," I said. "So try to concentrate. What the swamp monsters do is interesting, but it's not terribly exciting, even to paratellurian biologists who have carefully cultivated and nurtured a sense of wonder. If the indigenes couldn't do anything more exciting than that, they'd be freaks, but not particularly exciting freaks. I think they can do more. I think that they're unique even within this life-system, for very good evolutionary reasons.

"Doesn't it seem odd to you that all the other animal species, apart from the aliens who captured me, seem fairly primitive? Doesn't it seem to you that there's a yawning gap in the diversity of vertebrate forms?"

"Well," he said, "I suppose so. But it seems to me that perhaps the aliens are a bit more primitive than we assume. I don't doubt that they have a certain intelligence, at a very low level, but the artifacts they have aren't very much more sophisticated than the tools used by certain animal species on Earth. The fact that their nervous systems are complicated enough and sophisticated enough to have developed large brains is already accounted for in what you've said about investing in control over processes of metamorphosis. It seems to me that the aliens might be much more closely related to what you call the swamp monsters than is immediately obvious."

"That's reasonably good thinking," I told him, careful to keep him sweet. "But there's one thing that you aren't really taking into account—and that's your beloved central enigma: the question of *how* this facultative metamorphosis and multiple-structure potential is organized."

"I don't see any particular difficulty," he said. "It's just a matter of increased genetic potential. Like axolotls—only more so."

"In the case of the primitive animals—the swamp monsters—that may be so," I said. "But I think the *higher* vertebrates, a long time ago in the evolutionary past, developed a neater trick—a trick which increased their potential quite markedly."

"It can't have been much of a trick," he said, "if the higher vertebrates all died out except for the aliens themselves."

"That," I said confidently, "is where you're wrong. It's *because* it was such a neat trick that only one species of higher vertebrate exists today; and it's *because* it was such a neat trick that the lone species of higher vertebrate is much more dangerous than you imagine. The aliens may not be very sophisticated in technological terms, but in the sense that really matters—in terms of their biology—the indigenes aren't the primitives you imagine them to be. In a sense, they're more advanced than we are, and more advanced than we can ever become. So advanced that here on Naxos we couldn't even begin to compete with them."

"Go on," he said.

"Your central enigma," I reminded him, "wonders how it is that bodies come to have the complex structures that they do. It wonders how cells, which all have the same set of genes, become differentiated into hundreds of different types, all specifically located for collaboration in the organization of function. It wonders how an egg which has one set of coded instructions can divide repeatedly so that the bundle of cells it becomes get steadily more complicated and more highly-organized. The swamp-monsters seem to be even cleverer than we are, because their genetic systems not only have to organize the development of *one* organized structure but of several. That implies that their genetic apparatus must become more extensive and more highly organized itself. Presumably, there's a limit to that extension and organization, which means that swamp monsters can't really be all *that* versatile. Three or four stereotyped forms is probably all they can manage.

"But there's another kind of organization that a life-system like this one might be able to go in for. Suppose it was possible not simply to hold one genetic system complex enough to embody four different possible morphs. Suppose it was possible to have two different genetic systems, each one coding for a different morph, so that the organization of the manifest form could be passed from one integrated system to another."

"Okay," he said, "I've supposed it. So what?"

"It's not just a different kind of organization," I said. "It's a whole new ball game. Because along with it comes a whole new way for the organism to increase its metamorphic range. It no longer has to develop new forms by trial and error. It can work by co-opting new potentials. It can absorb new genetic systems whole. Your new brand of organism only has to develop *one* special trick—the trick which allows it to absorb other species and their genetic potentials into itself, to become gradually omnicompetent. The development of the 'higher vertebrates' here on Naxos was, in part, a matter of adaptive radiation and the development of new specializations. But there came a time when diversification was no longer a matter of the production of different species, because those species learned to fuse and recombine themselves into one single species that incorporated all the potentials the separate species had developed. It had to be that way—no other outcome was possible.

"The indigenes aren't just one more swamp-monster species, Simon. They're not just intelligent frogs. They're hundreds of species all rolled into one, and they have the capability to absorb into their own genetic potential the genetic potential of any new species that comes along—*including the genetic potential of a species from another life-system!* Because you see, Simon, although life here evolved in a way very different from life on Earth, there's still a very high degree of biochemical compatibility. At a fundamental level, our genetic *material* is very similar to theirs."

I stopped then, to let him work through the implications in his own mind. He wasn't quite as quick as me—after all, I'd a much fuller background in paratellurian biology than he had, and was better adapted in consequence to seeing possibilities—but he was clever enough.

"You mean," he said, "that those creatures could absorb the potentials of the human genetic system. They could add human form to their repertoire of metamorphoses."

"It's worse than that," I told him. "What I'm trying to get across to you is the fact that *they've already done it!*"

20

Catherine d'Orsay, needless to say, was much less ready to go for it. Even with the help of Simon Norton, we had a difficult job convincing her that what we were saying made sense. She tested its strength in every way she could.

"You're telling me," she said, "that the nineteen people in the dome were killed by an alien wearing human form."

"It's the one way that it all makes sense," said Angelina. "The woman whose corpse we never found must have been killed out there in the forest. They took her sterile suit, carved her up the way they carved Lee up, to drink blood and torn tissue through their fingertips. Then, having added her form to their repertoire, they sent one of their number back to the dome wearing her face and her suit."

"But even if I concede the physical transformation, this alien in disguise wouldn't be able to pass for human. It wouldn't be able to talk. It wouldn't even know how to open the dome."

"Think about it, captain," said Angelina, her voice almost pleading. "Opening the airlock doors is simple. There's no lock on them—nobody worries about the dome being invaded because they know that in order to get through both doors an invader has to pass through the sterilizing chamber. Anything not wearing a sterile suit is rendered very dead by the shower process. A *child* could open the doors. There doesn't have to be anyone else present, to issue a challenge or offer a greeting. All the alien had to do was pick its moment. Once inside the living quarters, the water tank is conveniently at hand. All it had to do was lift the lid and spit. Among their many other talents, the aliens have absorbed a defense mechanism which involves spitting venom. Once that was done, all it had to do was seal its suit up and walk out the same way it walked in. The aliens may be savages, but they're not stupid. Nothing we're attributing to them is outside their behavioral compass."

"Why did they do it?" asked the captain.

"Because it's their *modus operandi*. Absorb and destroy. Co-opt the potential of the enemy, and then destroy him, lest ye shall find thyself co-opted in thy turn. That's the law of life here. You could never make a peace treaty with natives like these—they're programed for a war of extinction."

"They didn't attempt to absorb the other members of the party. Why not?"

"They were betrayed by their assumptions. They thought they didn't have to. Once they'd used the poison, they couldn't—like some snakes back on Earth they're not immune to their own venom. They couldn't take in poisoned blood. They took for granted the fact that they only needed to absorb one set of genes—because, you see, there's no sexual differentiation on this world. There doesn't need to be, because the advantages it confers on Earthly species aren't applicable in this life-system, so far as the amphibians are concerned. The aliens are hermaphrodites, and they assumed that once they could make multiple copies of one human individual, they'd have the ability to breed in that particular morph, recombining and redistributing the genes. Incestuous, certainly, but possible— these individuals don't need to worry about hereditary defects in their offspring. . . . Their offspring just drop the defective morph from their repertoire. They didn't realize that in order to play recombination games with human genes, they'd need two complementary sets. By the time that became clear to them, it was too late for them to go after an Adam to pair with their Eve. Too late . . . until *we* arrived.

"Now they have everything they need. They can not only assume the appearance of human beings—they can breed in that morphological state. You see, captain, in a sense you—or rather *we*—have already colonized Naxos, in the only way that is or ever will be possible."

Catherine d'Orsay looked at me, and then at Zeno, as if to make sure that we were all in accord. Then she looked at Simon Norton, with an expression on her face which suggested that she believed him guilty of a terrible betrayal.

"This is crazy," she said.

"This is an alien life-system," I informed her. "It doesn't have to abide by our version of sanity."

"You don't have a single atom of proof that this is anything but a fantastic story."

"All we have," said Angelina steadily, "is the knowledge that it fits. And the conviction that it makes sense, genetically."

"You still have no proof. I have to have proof—you do see that, don't you?"

"Yes," I said sadly. "But you know what your proof is going to have to be, don't you?"

She considered, and then said, "If we could capture an alien . . ."

"Difficult," I said. "And maybe we could watch him for half a year without his turning into anything more homely than a big frog. *If* we could hold him that long."

She continued thinking, searching her imagination for a way to prove us wrong—if we *were* wrong—or to convince herself that we were right, if right we were.

"Captain," I said, "your people are walking around now in sterile suits. That gives them a measure of protection. How is it ever going to be possible to have people living normally on a world like this, if there's even a possibility that we might be right about the capabilities of this life-systm? There may be no infectious diseases that we can't handle, no deadly biochemical incompatibility between the local fruits and human stomachs. That isn't what counts here—it isn't what matters. You can't fight these aliens. If you meet them head on in a war of extermination, the probability is that you'll lose. They hold all the important advantages, and you have only firepower. You can't fight shapechangers, captain . . . and the war has already started. You know full well that if we're right, the proof will make itself manifest very shortly, when your people start getting killed. Are you going to wait for that to happen?"

She looked me in the eye, and her expression was

very grave as she gave her answer—the only answer, I suppose, that she *could* give.

She said, "I have to."

21

When we gave the explanation yet again, talking directly to Juhasz on the radio, we didn't get quite the hostile recpetion I was expecting. It seemed to be sinking into his consciousness that maybe we were more than just saboteurs, sent out by the evil governments of Earth to subvert his glorious mission. But he, too, was unsatisfied with what was still essentially a web of inspired guesses. He wanted an alien, dead and dissected, with these multiple talents displayed in a comprehensive account of its incredible physiology.

The trouble with fluid protoplasm, though, is that it decays far more rapidly than human cell structure. The rescue mission hadn't brought back an entire corpse from the scene of my epic battle, and the tissue samples they *had* collected were frustratingly uncommunicative when Zeno, Angelina and *Ariadne*'s biologists tried to agree on the significance of what they could divine of its properties. While these attempts to prove our case made little progress, Captain d'Orsay ordered that no one should ever be alone outside the dome, that an armed guard should be placed at both airlocks to challenge all who tried to enter, and that every man and woman should carry—and be prepared to use—a firearm.

Naturally, it wasn't enough.

Sometime during the second day of our attempt to find supporting evidence in the laboratory, two men disappeared. They had been sent to recover the remains of the aliens Angelina had shot. They had radios and maintained intermittent contact until they were in the vicinity of the crucial site. Then there was silence.

Catherine d'Orsay came to the sickroom to give me this news, and her face was ashen as she told me. I think she knew, then, that it was all over, and that I was going to be proven correct, but she couldn't admit it. She owed herself the certainty of final proof, and the *Ariadne* mission was too heavily committed now to be aborted without that proof being crystal clear.

She could have ordered everyone to stay in the dome, but she didn't. She knew that such a move would only lead to a delay in resolution. Instead, she stressed the need for absolute caution, and she waited for something unequivocal to emerge.

The next day, it happened. Two of the *Ariadne*'s crew—one a man and one a woman—were attacked by two persons wearing sterile suits. Mercifully, although the aliens now had two rifles, the attackers had no firearms. Perhaps it simply was not their way; perhaps they were not quite as intelligent as they might have been.

The woman was injured after a hand-to-hand encounter with one of the attackers, but the man was able to bring her back after the attackers had been put to flight. He was sure that both attackers were wounded by bullets, but they had nevertheless made good their escape. He would have tracked them, he said, were it not for his duty to his companion. Catherine d'Orsay's immediate reaction was to order out a hunting party, commissioned to follow the trail of the wounded aliens, but Angelina asked her to wait.

The injured woman was brought into the sick bay, and laid on a cot not far from mine.

Angelina asked the woman if she could recognize the face of the person who had attacked her, and she replied that she was sure that she could.

"Can you stand, Lee?" asked Angelina then of me.

I stood up, and hobbled on my wounded feet to stand at the head of the injured woman's bed. Catherine d'Orsay was present, watching carefully.

"Is this the face?" asked Angelina.

The woman's expression was quite unfathomable as she stared up at me.

"Yes," she said. "But when he attacked me, he didn't have that swollen nose."

"No," I said. "That's the legacy of experience, not genetics." I turned to Angelina and said: "It's lucky I'm so young. I still have the face that nature intended—more or less. At forty, so I'm told, people have the faces they deserve." To Catherine d'Orsay, I simply said: "Well?"

She tried to look impassive as she answered, but it was clear that her hopes had finally been consigned to the graveyard of dreams.

22.

We didn't strip the dome—instead we sealed it up in order to keep out prying eyes and hands. Someone would be back: not colonists, but someone. Simon Norton asked me if I might be among their number, and I said "Perhaps." It certainly wasn't beyond the bounds of possibility.

"It's not inconceivable," he said reflectively, "that we might learn to communicate with them and persuade them that there are advantages to peaceful cooperation."

"It's not impossible," I conceded, "but I for one wouldn't be happy teaching them a human language— though it would probably be much easier for them to master one than for us to master theirs. At present they can't *really* pass for human, but if they could...."

"Today Naxos," he murmured. "Tomorrow the universe."

I nodded.

"But if we could steal their children," he said, "and rear them according to *our* priorities, what might we not do with them?"

"We'd be preparing the way for our eventual destruction," I replied. "It might be a slower process than letting them infiltrate, but the result would be the same. They're too good. We couldn't control them."

He shook his head, and said: "I don't know." He was, by nature, an optimist.

"You don't have to stay with the *Ariadne*," I told him. "There's an empty berth on the *Earth Spirit*. Maybe you could come back here, if you wanted to."

He looked genuinely shocked. "We've lost far too many men as it is," he said. "Men and equipment. This mistake has cost us dearly. It isn't going to be easy, when we finally get to where we're going."

"Are you sure that you're going anywhere?" I asked. He was; there was no doubting it.

"Can you really stand to go back into the freezer now?" I went on. "Maybe another three hundred and fifty years before your next landfall. And when you get there, maybe another world like Naxos, attractive but deadly. There'll be no help then, you know. None of the three captains will license the lighting of another beacon. They'll make *Earth Spirit* a present of the one in orbit here, but Juhasz will consider that the cost of experience. If you think it's possible to persuade the shapeshifters of the benefits of mutual cooperation, why don't you even think it desirable to reach some accommodation with Earth?"

"I don't think you understand," he told me.

"No," I said, "I don't think I do. Let's call it an enigma."

And Simon, of course, was one of the saner ones. Once having accepted the inevitability, Catherine d'Orsay had quickly recovered her outward calm and authority, but how much the experience had cost her in terms of bankrupt emotional investment I couldn't judge. I spoke to her only once, and that briefly, before the shuttlecraft lifted.

"I'm sorry," I said, "that things turned out this way. I really am."

"You were never with us," she said colorlessly.

"No, but I was never against you. Juhasz was wrong in thinking that. He didn't need to dump us in the swamp. If he hadn't, though, things might have turned out worse. Even taking into account the fact that I was nearly flayed alive, I guess you could say that we were lucky. We jumped the right conclusion, and jumped it in a hurry. It might have taken a lot longer, and a lot more deaths. The original Ariadne died on Naxos, you know. Your mission came close to suffering the same fate.

"If we're trading allusions," she replied, "one might recall that Leander was killed one stormy night, trying unsuccessfully to reach an assignation with Hero."

That one stung, but I forgave her. She didn't know how close it was to the mark—the *Ariadne*'s people might be swapping rumors about my reciting John of Gaunt's speech, but nothing I'd said to Zeno and Angelina had been or ever would be repeated.

"The trouble with allusions," I said, "is that there never really is a true parallel. Your myth, you see, is missing Theseus—and it was Theseus, after all, that the story was all about. You could speak about the dark labyrinth between the stars, with just a little poetic license, but who were you guiding through it?"

She looked me in the eye, and without a flicker of expression she said: "Mankind."

"It's still wrong," I pointed out. "Theseus deserted Ariadne. In this case, it's *Ariadne* that's deserting—unless, of course, you do decide to plant another HSB if you ever reach a destination."

"You're right," she conceded, without a qualm. "It doesn't fit. If we've been deserted, it's only by people like Jason Harmall. But you might also remember that Ariadne's death on Naxos was only a brief intermission in her career. She eventually found her rightful place among the stars. Which is more than can be said for Leander."

I had to give it up. It was obvious that I couldn't

win. I never enjoyed the benefits of a classical education.

I didn't get to bandy words with Morten Juhasz after we got back to the *Ariadne*—a lost opportunity that I didn't much regret. There was one slightly edgy interview, though, between Angelina, myself and Jason Harmall.

It began well enough, with our thanking him for having played his part in getting me out of deep trouble with some of my skin still on my back. Then we apologized, for being such incompetent spies.

"But it didn't really matter, as things turned out," I observed. "Did it?"

"I think you might have made more of an effort," he purred.

"We might have," I agreed, "if we'd known exactly who and what we were supposed to be working for."

"Space Agency," he said, as if it were the most obvious thing in the world.

"No doubt," I replied. "But speaking for myself, I've been trying to work out exactly whose interests Space Agency is supposed to be promoting these days. If it's only doing what it's supposed to do, I don't see the necessity for a cloak-and-dagger section at all."

"Forget it, Lee," said Angelina. It was good counsel. A wise man would have accepted it, but I was still smarting from recent wounds, and my sense of discretion wasn't all that it might have been.

"We have more in common with the *Ariadne*'s people than is immediately obvious, haven't we?" I asked. By "we," of course, I meant Space Agency. I was entitled to call it "we," being a member in reasonably good standing, albeit at a low level. "They're declaring independence, deliberately taking what they imagine to be the fate of mankind into their own hands, taking the whole responsibility. Space Agency is doing the same, isn't it? Not that Marsbase and the satellites are going to declare their independence, of course—it's all just a *de facto* affair, achieved by information control. We're substituting our own goals for those of the governments of Earth, very quietly."

"Earth is stuck in a rut." said Harmall evenly. "It's too close to the brink of disaster, and it will never escape that brink. The only progress there's been for five hundred years has been progress in space. From the standpoint of the future, Dr. Caretta, *we* are mankind. Not just Space Agency—it's not as narrow as that. The offworld Soviets, too. It's not a rebellion, you know. It's just that we *are* the ones who are in control of destiny. It is, as you put it, simply a *de facto* affair. It's simply a matter of preventing Earth from exporting her problems into the universe."

"You amaze me," I said. I meant it literally. He smiled at me, as if I were simply being naïve, and the smile made me think I'd lost, though I hadn't really been arguing.

When he'd gone, I said to Angelina: "I bet Vesenkov's a better secret agent than we are."

"Probably," she replied.

We went to join Zeno for a sociable meal, so that he could explain to us how Naxos fitted into the great cosmic scheme. He'd already worked it all out; for him, there had to be some kind of metaphysical significance to it all, apart from playing silly games with mythological allusions, and I knew in advance that it wasn't going to be a hymn to the everlasting glory of humankind ... or even humanoidkind.

"All the other worlds which are possessed of what you call paratellurian biology," he pointed out, "are more violent and more changeable than Earth or Calicos. The disruptive forces against which life must contend in order to preserve its organization are that much greater, and life is simpler and more primitive in its accomplishments in consequence. Naxos is the first world we have found that is more stable than Earth and Calicos, where the life-system is *not* in contention with forces even as violent as those which operate on our homeworlds. It may be that for every world like Calicos in the universe at large, there is also a world like Naxos. Our hopes of expansion into the galaxy, and domination of its spaces, may be more fragile than we have so far imagined."

"Not really," I told him. "The shapeshifters may be cleverer than we are—maybe you could say that they were much better adapted to their environment. That doesn't mean that they'd ever become competitors. You could argue that *because* they're much better adapted to their immediate environment, they have no incentive to leave it. From *our* point of view they may not be living in paradise, but from their viewpoint life is comfortable."

"Passing space travelers would have said the same about your own remote ancestors," he countered. "And in any case, such innocence as the men of Naxos once possessed is shattered now. There is a serpent in their Eden, and if they are to come to terms with it, they must make progress—*our* kind of progress. We have seen the future, Lee, and it does not belong to beings like us. We are transients in the universe, the products of a sidetracked evolutionary process. If it is not the men of Naxos who will come into the inheritance we hoped might be ours, it will be creatures more akin to them than to us. We would be blind if we did not recognize the significance of what we have learned about life in these last few days."

"It won't affect our lives," I pointed out. "We can cherish our illusions while we pass our time here—just as the captains of the *Ariadne* can."

"Certainly," said Zeno. "But the point is that we know them to be illusions. We know that we are merely pawns in a game whose settlement is beyond our scope."

"We always knew that," I said. "Didn't we?"

23

We spent a couple of days on the *Ariadne* before her crew were ready to place themselves once more in suspended animation; before the ship herself was lifted by the intoxication of a dream and carried away toward the distant stars. They were slow days for all of us, I think. What was good about them—at least from my point of view—was that there was room to move and breathe, and to enjoy a little privacy. I wasn't looking forward to the long trip home in the cramped quarters of the *Earth Spirit*. It didn't promise ideal circumstances for my gradual recovery from the multiple injuries inflicted upon me during my stay on Naxos.

On the second day, the Hyper-Spatial Beacon was re-ignited, to restore an important stepping stone in mankind's attempt to conquer the universe.

It was quite an emotional moment.

When all the farewells were over, Angelina said, "I suppose if I were to kiss you, you'd have bad dreams, and you'd be sure to have wiped it from your memory by the time you woke up."

"I don't know," I said, "but we could try."

So we did, and it had no adverse effects at all.

End of nightmare?

Well perhaps.